NO WAY HOME

(A Carly See FBI Suspense Thriller—Book 3)

Rylie Dark

Rylie Dark

Bestselling author Rylie Dark is author of the SADIE PRICE FBI SUSPENSE THRILLER series, comprising six books (and counting); the MIA NORTH FBI SUSPENSE THRILLER series, comprising six books (and counting); the CARLY SEE FBI SUSPENSE THRILLER, comprising six books (and counting); and the MORGAN STARK FBI SUSPENSE THRILLER, comprising three books (and counting).

An avid reader and lifelong fan of the mystery and thriller genres, Rylie loves to hear from you, so please feel free to visit www.ryliedark.com to learn more and stay in touch.

ISBN: 978-1-0943-9525-8

BOOKS BY RYLIE DARK

SADIE PRICE FBI SUSPENSE THRILLER
ONLY MURDER (Book #1)
ONLY RAGE (Book #2)
ONLY HIS (Book #3)
ONLY ONCE (Book #4)
ONLY SPITE (Book #5)
ONLY MADNESS (Book #6)

MIA NORTH FBI SUSPENSE THRILLER
SEE HER RUN (Book #1)
SEE HER HIDE (Book #2)
SEE HER SCREAM (Book #3)
SEE HER VANISH (Book #4)
SEE HER GONE (Book #5)
SEE HER DEAD (Book #6)

CARLY SEE FBI SUSPENSE THRILLER
NO WAY OUT (Book #1)
NO WAY BACK (Book #2)
NO WAY HOME (Book #3)
NO WAY LEFT (Book #4)
NO WAY UP (Book #5)
NO WAY TO DIE (Book #6)

MORGAN STARK FBI SUSPENSE THRILLER
TOO LATE (Book #1)
TOO CLOSE (Book #2)
TOO FAR GONE (Book #3)

PROLOGUE

Sarah Tooley awoke to the sound of a low, whispering voice in the dark.

"Don't move."

Sarah didn't immediately know where she was. She reflexively twitched and heard the voice again.

"Don't move, I said. I don't want this to be painful."

Sarah froze in place, struggling to clear her mind.

I'm at home, she realized. *In bed. I was fast asleep.*

She felt the icy chill of fear creep over her body.

Then she became aware of a sharp point touching her throat.

A knife.

She didn't dare move. Whoever it was could slash her throat in an instant if he chose to do so.

A question formed on Sarah's lips:

"What do you want from me?"

But she didn't speak the words aloud. The answer seemed horrifyingly clear. She was alone in bed in her apartment at night, and an intruder was holding a blade at her throat.

It wasn't hard to guess what the intruder intended to do to her.

"Please don't do this," she said in a voice that was hoarse with sleep and fear. "Please don't."

The man let out a small gasp of surprise.

"Do you think I want to … ?"

His voice faded for a moment.

"No, no, I wouldn't think of *that.* Please don't worry, I don't mean you any harm. But you really mustn't move. This blade is extremely sharp. I don't want to cut your windpipe. That would be terrible, Sarah. You would suffer."

He knows my name.

She was almost as puzzled as she was terrified. The man's face was shadowy but visible in the dim light that spilled in through her apartment window. His expression was gentle, and his eyes were crinkled in a slight smile. And there was something familiar about him, although she couldn't remember from where or when.

Have I heard this voice before?

Or is it just his face?

She didn't know.

Somehow, though, his expression was all the more frightening for seeming almost friendly—frightening and grotesque and wrong.

"Listen," the man whispered.

Listen to what?

Then she realized—the couple who lived next door were shouting at each other, and their baby was crying. They argued a lot, and Sarah could always hear it through the flimsy wall that separated their apartments—although lately she'd gotten so accustomed to their late-night quarreling that she sometimes fell fast asleep even while it was going on.

The man tilted his head.

"I can't make out their words, can you?"

Sarah couldn't either, but she didn't risk a reply. Though often painfully loud, the couple's voices were always too muffled for her to hear exactly what they were shouting at each other, except for an explosive obscenity now and then.

The man sighed sympathetically.

"What tragic lives those two must live," he said. "And the baby too. What chance has the poor child in life, growing up around so much anger? So much hate? The cycle will repeat itself again and again, generation after generation."

He listened intently for a moment, then added, "Such a shame there's nobody to stop it."

For the first time since this ordeal had begun, Sarah fleetingly wondered whether she might be dreaming. Her assailant's words echoed her own frequent thoughts about the quarreling couple. She'd even said as much to her husband.

"I feel so sorry for them, Scott," she'd said.

But Scott never shared her sympathy. He had a temper of his own, and when he heard the couple quarreling, he'd often charge down the hall and pound on the door and yell at them to shut up. A shouting match would ensue between Scott and the man inside, and other neighbors would start poking their heads through their doors to complain about the racket and …

Scott!

Sarah suddenly thought of something she needed to say.

"My husband will be back at any minute."

The man looked disappointed as he shook his head.

"Oh, Sarah, Sarah, please don't lie to me."

"I—I'm not lying."

"You are. I know perfectly well that Scott works the midnight-to-eight shift at the Saunders Building. He won't be here for hours. It's really hurtful to lie to me like that."

Sarah was terrified into complete silence again. The noise on the other side of the wall continued.

The man tilted his head curiously.

"What are their names?"

It took a moment for her to understand that he was asking about her neighbors.

"I—I don't know," she stammered.

The man's eyes widened.

"You don't know the names of your next door neighbors?"

"No."

"Don't you have any friends at all here in this building?"

Sarah didn't reply for a moment. For some reason, it was hard for her to admit the truth.

His voice was so compassionate that Sarah almost relaxed a little.

"Please tell me," he urged in a comforting tone. "I really want to know."

Maybe he really doesn't mean me any harm.

But then, why was he still holding the point of a blade at her throat?

"Scott and I don't know anybody here," she finally blurted.

"Such a shame. But that's what life is like in these low-rent apartment buildings, isn't it? So cold and impersonal. Everybody is half-afraid to make eye contact with anybody else. That must be very hard for you—especially since you and Scott scarcely ever see each other, with him working nights and you working days. You must be putting in—what?—45 or 50 hours a week at that gift shop."

Sarah felt a new surge of panic.

He knows where I work.

He even knew how much she worked.

Again, she felt as though his face was somehow familiar.

The man stroked her hair with his free hand.

"But soon all that will be over. Soon you'll be with Amber."

Amber! Sarah thought with a shudder.

She felt a stab of grief as well as horror at the mention of the name. Amber Jordan had been her best friend since childhood. But she'd died a slow, lingering, painful death from leukemia about a month ago.

Sarah became dimly aware of the man reaching into his pocket for something with his free hand.

"I'm going to give you something very important," he told her. "Whatever you do, you mustn't let go of it. You will need it, I promise you."

He pushed something hard and round into the palm of her hand—a coin, Sarah thought. Then he closed her fingers around it. Then he moved the knife around to the side of her throat.

"This doesn't have to hurt much. No worse than cutting your finger, really—and only for a moment."

Sarah suddenly felt a swift, sharp pain at her throat. Then she felt a pulsating spray of blood.

Her own blood.

She tried to thrash loose, but the man held her down with a single strong hand in the center of her chest.

She felt too weak to put up a struggle.

Then came a wild dizziness, almost like being drunk.

Numbness swept through her body.

He's right. It really doesn't hurt.

She felt on the verge of remembering where she'd seen that face.

But she lost consciousness before that could happen.

CHAPTER ONE

As the little cabin cruiser lurched and skidded over rough waters, Carly See hung onto her bench in the open stern. She was just as glad that the motor was too noisy for casual conversation. Before they'd left, the pilot had been plenty curious about why she was hiring him for this trip. Now he had settled into navigating toward their destination.

She felt a chill as the islands came into sight—and not just from the cold wind and the spray of icy saltwater stinging her face.

It was a chill of recognition.

She'd seen those same sharp peaks and cliffs twice before in her life. The first time was as a little girl, when her parents brought Carly and her sister on vacation to California. They had gone out on a tour boat to see whales, dolphins, and other wildlife that inhabited this area.

"Oh, the dolphins!" little Megan had cried out. *"Look at the dolphins!"*

The second time Carly had seen the tall central peak and the smaller ones beside it, she hadn't actually been looking at them across open water. Two days ago, she had glimpsed those islands in a vision that replicated her childhood adventure.

She knew the image had to be important, because her visions were not a product of her imagination.

They were messages from the dead.

Images and words sometimes flowed freely to her from those no longer living. The hard part was figuring out what those messages meant. In spite of that difficulty, and the necessity to hide her ability from others, those communications had helped her solve many mysteries.

The boat slowed as it neared a single narrow dock that extended out from a rocky beach. Close up, the jagged peaks of Santa Novara looked even sharper than Carly had remembered. It was hard to believe that the islands were even inhabited. But she could see clusters of white-chested birds high up on those rocks and some brown animals lolling about on a small beach. Three small clapboard houses at the base of the cliffs indicated that humans also lived here.

Carly wanted to find out who lived here. Might her sister be among them, alive and well? If so, where had she been during all the years since she'd gone missing? If Megan wasn't here, might the people have some idea where she was now? Since Carly only heard from the spirits of the dead, she shuddered at the possibility of actually hearing from Megan's spirit while she was here.

She can't be dead, she thought. *She just can't be.*

She pulled off her scarf and patted her head. Although a few strands of her long dark hair had come free from the bun she wore while working, she decided it would have to do.

The pilot pulled his boat to a halt at the pier, then climbed out to tie his mooring lines. A gangly man with long red hair and a beard came striding toward them. He hurried out onto the dock and helped Carly out of the boat.

"Special Agent Carly See, I assume," he said.

"And you must be Curtis Novak."

The man wagged his finger at her.

"*Dr.* Curtis Novak, the director of the Novara Marine Research Center."

Then with a rakish smile, he added, "But I guess you can call me Curt. Everybody else here does."

The pilot spoke to Carly as he finished mooring the boat.

"I'll wait here for you."

"It's not too cold?"

"Nope. I'll be fine right here."

With that he ducked inside the boat's little cabin and closed the door.

Carly and Curt walked along the dock to the rocky shore. The island air was scarcely less damp and cold than it had been on the boat, and it was just early October. Carly could only imagine how harsh the weather would get here as winter set in.

"I must say, Agent See, you've piqued my curiosity," Curt said. "You seem to be here on some mysterious errand. I hope you can tell me what this is all about."

Carly hesitated. She wasn't exactly proud of how she'd managed to obtain his permission to come to this place where only scientists were usually allowed. Back in Virginia, she'd sent him a cryptic email:

I am Special Agent Carly See of the FBI's Behavioral Analysis Unit. I am working on a missing person case that might involve your research facility. I am not at liberty to say more at this time, but I hope

I may visit you at Santa Novara tomorrow to discuss this face to face. Please acknowledge your permission in your reply.

She'd signed her name and also attached her official identification to the email. Dr. Curtis Novak had responded almost immediately, making an appointment with Carly without asking any questions.

But now she was going to have to tell the truth. She took a deep breath and gathered up the courage to admit to her deception.

"Curt, I'm afraid I'm not really here on FBI business."

"You're not looking for a missing person?"

"Actually, that part is true, but ..."

Her voice faded for a moment.

"The missing person in question is my sister, Megan See."

Curt squinted at her as they walked along.

"So this is purely a personal thing for you?"

"That's right."

"And your superiors have no idea you're here, I suppose."

"I'm afraid not."

"And I guess you'd wind up in quite a lot of trouble if I reported how you used your official status as a ruse to visit a scientific facility that's completely off limits to the public."

Carly swallowed hard. She stopped walking for a moment and turned her gray eyes directly on him.

"You're right about that, Curt. And I wouldn't blame you if you did report me. But the truth is, I'm not sure I'd care. I'd do just about anything to find out what happened to Megan. And I don't care much about the consequences."

Curt chuckled and patted Carly on the arm. As he resumed walking toward the houses, she followed along beside him.

"That's the spirit," he told her. "That's the kind of determination I like to hear. And it's kind of nice to get a little human drama on this island for a change. We humans here are vastly outnumbered, as you can see."

He pointed to various groups of wildlife on the beach and cliffs.

"We've got every kind of seal you can think of—northern elephant seals, harbor seals, California sea lions. And we've got maybe a quarter of a million sea birds of one kind or another. This sanctuary is dedicated to them, and they tolerate our human presence. We do our best not to wear out our welcome."

Carly peered at the black-and-white birds up on the cliffs.

"Are those penguins?" she asked.

"No, but they look like it from a distance. Those are common murres, and they can fly just fine. I can give you a hiking tour of the island if you've got time."

The offer was almost tempting. But she'd taken advantage of a little downtime from her job to fly all the way out here, and she really needed to catch a plane home at the San Francisco International Airport tonight. Besides, she'd also spent way more on this trip than she could afford.

"I'm afraid I can't stay that long," she said.

"OK, let's get down to business. First of all, let's get you out of this cold air. I'm sure you're not used to it."

They walked into one of the small houses and into a snug, dry office. Curt poured Carly a hot cup of tea, which offered welcome warmth to her hands and her throat. Curt sat down facing her across his desk.

"I hate to say this, Agent See," he said, "but I'm afraid you've wasted your trip. We've got a total of six human beings living on this island, and none of them are named Megan See."

"Do you think she might have lived here in the past?"

Curt was scrolling on his computer screen now.

"When did she go missing?" he asked.

"About ten years ago."

"That's a long time."

"I know."

Carly could see a list of names reflected in his glasses.

"That name doesn't show up in our records. And this a list of everybody who has lived here since long before you say she disappeared."

"Might she have worked here under an assumed name?"

"I don't see how that's possible. She'd have to be a naturalist or a scientist in some related field, and our researchers are very carefully screened. Their credentials have to be exceptional, and they also have to be who they say they are. Do you have a picture of her?"

Carly produced one of the last pictures she had of her sister and showed it to him.

Curtis shrugged and shook his head.

"That face doesn't look familiar. And I haven't seen many different faces in a long time, not in the six years I've worked here. I'd recognize her if I'd ever seen her, even if she'd come here just for a short-term project."

Carly's heart sank, and she silently berated herself.

I shouldn't have gotten my hopes up, she thought.

After all, there had surely never been much likelihood of Megan being on this island with a bunch of scientists.

Curt looked away from his computer and swiveled his chair toward her.

"Carly—do you mind if I call you Carly, since you're not exactly here in an official capacity?"

"Please do."

"Tell me, Carly—what reason do you have for thinking she might have been here?"

Carly stifled a sigh. She'd been half-hoping he wasn't going to ask her that question. But of course she knew it was inevitable.

"Curt, if I tell you, you'll think I'm crazy."

He laughed.

"Carly, I'm afraid that ship has sailed, so to speak. Right now I've got no reason to think you're in your right mind. Go on and tell me."

Maybe he'd actually believe me, she thought.

But how could she tell this man a secret that she'd scarcely breathed to another human soul—not even her BAU partner?

"I'm afraid I can't do that," she finally said.

Curt shrugged and folded his hands together on his desktop.

"Then what can you seriously expect me to do?" he asked.

"Can I talk to the others? The researchers who live here, I mean?"

Carly more than half-expected the man to say no. Instead, he sent a text message to the five other people on the island, and within a few minutes they had all gathered in the office.

*

After only a few questions, Carly realized that none of the researchers had any knowledge of her sister's whereabouts. They were a colorful group, all scruffy and weather-beaten, and they all had "doctor" in front of their names.

Carly guessed that Curt had only let her talk to them as a diversion, an amusing and bemusing novelty for a group of people with scant contact with the world beyond the island. The researchers seemed far more curious about her than she could ever be about them. They also seemed remarkably sympathetic.

But it's definitely time to leave, she realized.

The group returned to their various posts and tasks, and Curt accompanied Carly back to the dock. On their way there, Carly noticed how narrow the beaches were, and how dark the sand was.

"Are there any wider beaches on this island?" she asked Curt. "With whiter sand?"

"No, it's all like this, like a big rock came popping out of the ocean. Which is probably pretty nearly what happened all those millions of years ago."

Carly realized that the last of her hopes were crushed.

Weeks had passed since the first vision that led her to believe her sister was alive. In that one, Megan had been walking on a wide beach with beautiful white sand.

Megan was never here.

The beach she'd seen her sister on might have been anywhere. And apparently her more recent vision of this island seen from open water hadn't been helpful either. Carly hadn't felt even the slightest hint of any spirit reaching out to her since she'd come here.

Her trip was utterly pointless.

In a matter of moments, Carly was riding the boat back to San Francisco, struggling with questions that wouldn't leave her alone. If those jagged islands had no meaning, why had she seen them at all? Was she supposed to try to find information about the tour boat her family had taken all those years ago, or someone else who had been on that tour, or some other beach along the California coast?

Her heart sank as she remembered one more thing about Santa Novara.

Native Americans had called them *Islands of the Dead.*

Was that all she was supposed to learn from the vision?

Whenever she'd received visions regarding Megan, they'd never come directly from Megan herself, but from a long-dead childhood friend who seemed to know something about Megan's whereabouts. Carly found this comforting in a way, because she never received messages from the living, only from the dead. As long as she didn't hear from Megan directly, there was still a chance her sister was alive.

Unless …

The Islands of the Dead.

The name itself was deeply unsettling. Was she wrong to believe that she could find her sister still alive somewhere?

Maybe I'll never know.

As if to remind her that it was time for her to return to her regular life, her phone buzzed. Her spirits lifted slightly when she saw who had texted her. The message even made her smile just a little.

What do you say to tomorrow for lunch?

At least she had something to look forward to when she got back to Virginia.

CHAPTER TWO

Carly examined her face in the mirror, checking carefully under her eyes for any sagging that showed how little sleep she'd gotten recently. She'd spent 14 hours on planes plus time in taxis and a boat just for that fruitless excursion to Santa Novara.

I don't look too bad, she told herself.

Even at age 30, she liked to think she "cleaned up" pretty well after the down and dirty work on serial murder cases. But today she wasn't getting ready for FBI fieldwork or even for office tasks at Quantico.

She wouldn't be pulling her long dark hair back into a bun.

Today she would let her hair hang free, and she had to find something especially attractive to wear.

The text she'd received yesterday was from Mark Lawson, her long-ago high school boyfriend. He was in D.C. for a convention and wanted to get together for lunch.

She had responded,

I'd like that. What do you have in mind?

They had agreed on a time and place, and now she had to get dressed and drive from her Virginia apartment into the city in time to meet him.

Carly was looking forward to their date …

If that's what it is.

Their relationship status was extremely uncertain right now. Maybe today they'd get a better idea of where things stood between them.

Her thoughts were interrupted by her phone buzzing on the bathroom counter.

Lyle! she realized, picking up the phone.

She hadn't talked to her BAU partner since the debriefing from their most recent case. Lyle hadn't looked at all well at the time, and with good reason. He'd barely escaped death at the hands of a serial killer who had injected him with a paralytic drug. It was a drug that was used in some surgeries—a neuromuscular blocking agent, the doctors called it. Lyle had been ordered to take time off for full recovery, and

Carly had been granted a few free days as well.

"Hey, Lyle. How're you resting up?" she asked him. As they talked, Carly wandered to her kitchen, picked up a mug of coffee, and then sat down on her couch.

"I'm done resting up. I'm bored. How about you?"

Carly was a bit surprised by his somewhat snappish tone.

"I'm, uh, kind of looking forward to a few more free days," she said.

"Well, I'm glad *one* of us is. What have you been doing with your time, anyhow?"

Carly felt brought up short. She couldn't think of any plausible excuse for having flown out to California and back. It certainly hadn't been restful. Although she valued honesty in their relationship, there were things she hadn't told him about herself. Telling him about her trip to California would mean revealing the riddling communications she'd received from the dead. Her partner didn't know about her peculiar gift, and she didn't think he was ready to hear it.

"Oh, you know," she answered vaguely. "Just resting and recuperating."

"Well, no more of that for me. I'm ready for another case. I'm gnashing at the bit."

Carly fell silent for a moment, remembering that terrifying interval when Lyle lay physically helpless at the mercy of the killer.

She stammered in reply, "Uh, Lyle, don't forget what the Quantico doctor told you about getting back to work too early."

"Yeah, yeah, yeah. The aftereffects of vecuronium might linger for a while, and I ought to get some serious rest, and blah-blah-blah."

"Maybe you should think seriously about that."

"I've lived long enough to know that work is the best therapy for me. What do you say we get back in action? I want to give Voss a call and see if anything is up."

Carly fell silent again. Special Agent Preston Voss was their team chief at Quantico, and he usually assigned them their cases. Part of Carly thought she should flat-out say that this was a bad idea. But judging from her partner's prickly tone, she thought an argument might well follow.

Maybe Voss won't have any open cases, she thought.

Better yet, maybe Voss would talk sense into Lyle about his need to decompress for a while.

It's not like he'll listen to me.

"I guess it's OK," Carly muttered.

"You *guess?* Where's your enthusiasm, Carly?"

"I said OK."

"Great. I'll get back to you whenever I know something."

Lyle ended the call, and Carly sat staring at the phone in her hand. Her partner's tone had her worried.

He sounds desperate.

While it was true they'd just closed a dangerous case which had almost gotten both of them killed, the same had been true of many of their other cases. So why did he sound so shaky right now?

Carly knew it must have been terrifying for him to be helplessly paralyzed. After something like that, maybe she, too, would feel anxious to get back to work and put the trauma behind her.

But all that was out of her hands. Right now, she had to go find something exciting to wear.

I do have a lunch date, she told herself with a slight giggle.

And for the moment, at least, she wasn't working on a murder case.

*

The man took a deep breath as he stepped inside the Garrison Funeral Home.

He sighed with pleasure as he exhaled.

"Ahhhh."

Although it was a lovely fall day outside, he definitely preferred this kind of atmosphere. There was something about the air in a good funeral home always that seemed fresh and especially clean to him, and even cheerful.

The interior of the Garrison Funeral Home didn't look all that different from other such places in Harmonium. The front lobby connected with four visitation rooms and a large chapel at the far end. The decor resembled a luxury hotel, with pristine furniture, patterned carpeting, and soothing, pastel-colored wall paneling

Even so, he found the Garrison Funeral Home uniquely pleasant. There was something ineffably serene about the ambience of the place.

The dead are treated well here.

Bodies were never handled casually or callously here. Great care was taken in their embalming and restoration, making them look mysteriously alive and more in harmony with the world than they likely ever were in life.

That care and sensitivity rubbed off on friends and family of the dead.

This is a happy place.

As he peeked into one of the visitation rooms, he saw a black-clad woman standing alone over an open coffin. She was dabbing her face a little as she looked down at the man's body inside it—her late husband, the man guessed. But her features were relaxed, tranquil, even beatific, as if she were happy that her husband had finished his days of pain and tribulation and was on his way to a peaceful hereafter.

These surroundings were designed to have such an effect on mourners.

It helps people see things as they really are.

As he approached the arched doorway leading into another visitation room, he was a bit startled to hear the sound of chuckling. He peeked inside and saw a man and a woman sitting in front of an open coffin with a young man inside. They were whispering and laughing with their heads close together until they noticed someone looking in on them.

They suddenly pulled away and blushed with embarrassment, but nevertheless couldn't quite stifle a remnant of the giggles.

The man smiled at them.

They needn't be embarrassed as far as he was concerned.

Life goes on.

One of the great purposes of an open casket was to prove that very point.

And the couple's merriment wasn't the least bit mean or contemptuous, but palpably sweet and loving.

They were obviously sharing a joke they had once shared with the dead man.

And he's laughing too, I'm sure.

All was well in the mystic sphere these living shared with their dead.

But then the man became aware of a bitter, discordant voice coming from the chapel at the far end of the foyer. He hurried there and quietly slipped inside the double doors.

A funeral was in progress.

In an open coffin at the front of the chapel was a woman in her 30s. Even from here the man could see that the mortician's best efforts hadn't been able to erase telltale signs of strain, pain, and hardship the deceased had suffered during her short life.

Sometimes the dead are beyond mortal help, he thought.

Less than a dozen people were seated in the rows of chairs, looking bored and restless. One woman was actually fanning herself with the service program, despite the fact that the temperature here was perfectly comfortable.

A pastor with a white collar stood listening while a woman stood speaking at the podium. The man knew the pastor—his name was Miles Lindsay. The man knew what sort of man Pastor Lindsay was, and the sorts of things he was capable of.

Not a good man.

The man pitied Lindsay's flock for being so thoroughly taken in by him.

As for the woman who was speaking, she looked close to the same age as the deceased. Her face looked tired, sorrowful, and even angry.

The man paused to listen to what she was saying.

"… and to tell the truth, I don't know what any of you are doing here today. None of you bothered to give my sister the time of day after her accident. Her helplessness was just too … inconvenient, I guess. None of you gave me any help during the 15 years I spent taking care of her, seeing to her every need. But here you are for some reason …"

She fell silent with a choking sob of rage, then resumed.

"And now that Lisa is gone, I've got nothing. No reason to go on. And none of you care about me, any more than you did about Lisa. And you know what? I envy her. She's through with you, and with life, and I wish I were through with it all too."

A man stood up and walked toward her and half-heartedly tried to put his arms around her, but she pushed him away and sat down apart from the others. Despite a discontented murmur, the seated people seemed pretty much unfazed by the woman's tirade. One man looked at his watch.

The pastor stepped up to the podium and began to make his concluding remarks.

The poor woman, the man thought.

She needs my help—just like the others did.

He made up his mind to wait right here for her, so he could introduce himself and get to know her just a little.

Soon her suffering will be over, he thought.

Meanwhile, he fingered the bright new penny in his pants pocket.

She'll be needing this, he thought.

CHAPTER THREE

Her high heels almost tripped Carly up when she got out of her car in a Washington, D.C., parking garage. She stopped for a moment and steadied herself.

You can't have forgotten how to do every ordinary thing, she thought anxiously.

It seemed a long time since she'd worn anything but sturdy flats and slacks, which were certainly best for checking out crime scenes or running down suspects. But today she'd put on a long-sleeved blue dress that draped nicely around her lean body and was short enough to show off her legs. Since she was going directly from the parking garage into the Kingman Hotel where Mark Lawson's convention was being held, she didn't even need a jacket.

Walking more gracefully now, Carly made her way to the hotel restaurant, where she was a bit alarmed to see linen tablecloths and silverware rolled up in cloth napkins.

Definitely out of my price range.

Before the host could approach to ask her if she had a reservation, she saw Mark stand up at one of the tables and give her a jaunty wave. With his three-piece suit, robin's-egg-blue silk shirt, and matching handkerchief tucked neatly into his jacket pocket, Mark looked more at home in this setting than she felt.

"That's my friend waiting for me," she told the host.

She walked on into the restaurant, quite naturally she thought. Mark looked appreciative as he held out a chair for her, but then he appeared unsure about his display of old-school gallantry.

"Uh, I hope this doesn't strike you as 'caveman' behavior," he joked.

"Not at all."

Although the truth was, she wasn't used this sort of courtesy and wasn't really comfortable with it.

Mark helped her into her seat and then sat down across from her. Before they could start making conversation, a white-shirted waiter with a black bow tie came up to their table and asked if they were ready to order.

"Give us just a minute," Mark replied.

After one look at the menu, Carly felt daunted by the prices. Mark apparently noticed her uneasiness.

"Don't worry, I'm paying," he said. "I'm a big-city lawyer, remember?"

Carly smiled at his little joke. Mark had a law office in Carly's small hometown of Currie, Illinois—the largest law office in town, but a small one, nonetheless. She had seen him very briefly last month when she'd been in Currie to visit her parents. But before that, it had been about ten years since they'd gotten together.

She felt a surge of admiration for his familiar strong features, blue eyes, and neatly combed-back brown hair. But she could also see the changes the past decade had made. Mark wore glasses now, and gone was the sweetly enthusiastic expression from high school days. He looked serious and rather tired—partly due to a failed marriage, Carly knew.

I wonder how I look to him?

Carly worried a little as she perused the menu. She didn't want to order anything overly expensive, but she also knew Mark would feel awkward if she went out of her way to order something glaringly inexpensive, like a simple appetizer.

She finally decided on a serving of fettuccini carbonara, while Mark chose a pork tenderloin sandwich. The waiter took their order and quickly brought each of them a glass of house wine.

After they each took a sip, Mark asked, "So are you getting rested after your last case?"

Carly couldn't help chuckling a little. Her trip to California and back had hardly been restful, but she wasn't ready to talk about all that.

"I guess I'm trying."

"Your last case was in New Mexico, wasn't it? I saw something about it in the news, but it was all rather vague. A serial killer posing his victims to look like statues?"

"Something like that. The killer was a psychopathic misogynist who wanted to make an exhibit of sculptures based on his victims. He made bronze death masks of their faces."

"That's bizarre. Was it dangerous? For you, I mean?"

From his earnest tone and his crinkled expression, she realized he wasn't just trying to make conversation.

He really wants to know.

But Carly couldn't bring herself to talk about how close both she and Lyle had come to getting killed, much less how often their cases put them in mortal danger. She hoped he wasn't going to press the issue.

"Uh, I'd rather talk about what you've been up to, Mark."

Finally he just shrugged.

"Well, the convention is proving to be … interesting."

He paused and drummed his fingers on the table.

"I got an offer to join a criminal law firm right here in Washington."

Carly felt her jaw drop a little.

"Wow, that's …"

"Yeah, it's quite a development. It would be a whole new thing for me. I mean, there isn't much call for criminal trial law in Currie. I'm used to doing family law, civil litigation, estate planning, municipal cases, all that kind of stuff, but …"

He fell silent again for a moment.

"But I think maybe I feel ready for a change."

"I hope it works out for you."

"We'll see."

Another silence fell.

"What about you, Carly?" Mark finally asked.

"What do you mean?"

He reached across the table for Carly's hand.

"If I move out here, we'll practically be neighbors again. Would it be … OK with you if we saw a lot more of each other?"

Carly felt brought up short again. This city was large, and she was often on assignment in other parts of the country. Actually, they could still go for years without seeing each other.

Unless we make an effort to get together.

"This sounds like an incredible opportunity," she said. "I don't see how you can possibly turn it down."

"That's not exactly what I'm asking."

"I know."

She gave his hand an affectionate squeeze.

"Seeing each other after all these years brings back a lot of emotions, doesn't it?" she said.

"And a lot of memories, too," Mark said with a nod.

As they just sat and looked at each other for a few moments, Carly let herself get swept into those emotions and memories. Holding his hand reminded her of how they used to sit together on the porch swing of her family home for hours on end, talking endlessly about the future.

"We had a lot of dreams back then," she said.

"We sure did."

Mark had wanted to become a great writer. Carly had been starting to dream of a career in law enforcement, but she had also fantasized about traveling to faraway places.

Then something happened ...

Megan's disappearance had derailed their budding romance. Carly, Mark, and Megan had spent a lot of time together, and Mark had actually taken the last photograph Carly had of herself with her sister. It showed them happily eating cotton candy together at a carnival.

Mark and Carly had broken up soon after Megan's disappearance. At the time, neither one of them knew exactly why. But over the years, Carly had come to understand. With so many painful questions about that terrible loss, they just couldn't enjoy being around each other anymore.

As if reading her thoughts, Mark shrugged sadly.

"There are three people here at this table, aren't there?" he said.

A little startled at his perception, Carly felt her eyes welling up with tears.

The waiter rescued them from those sharp memories by bringing their meals. Then it was easier to talk about less difficult topics—mostly about Mark's life in Currie and the kinds of cases a small town lawyer handled, and also the latest gossip about people Carly hadn't seen for years. It was pleasant, and both of them wound up laughing from time to time.

Soon they finished their entrees, and the waiter came and took their plates and gave them dessert menus. As Carly perused the offerings, she found herself veering closer to telling Mark the truth about herself—and why she believed that Megan might be alive. Maybe she'd start by telling him about yesterday's fruitless trip to Santa Novara.

But before the waiter could come back to take their dessert order, Carly's phone rang.

It gave her a jolt to see that the call was from Special Agent Voss himself.

I guess Lyle must have called Voss, like he said he would.

"I've got to take this," she told Mark.

"OK."

She got up and stepped a short distance away from the table.

"How have you been doing since the New Mexico case?" Voss

asked her.

"Fine."

"Do you feel up to taking a new case?"

"Yes, I do."

She heard a hint of a sigh and realized that Voss wasn't completely happy with her answer.

"OK, then. How soon can you be in my office?"

"In a little over an hour."

"Be ready to travel."

Voss ended the call. Carly's mind was already racing as she returned to the table. It seemed ludicrous that she had to go to a job when she'd dressed for a date. But she knew that her go-bag was always in her car with a change of clothes and everything else she might need.

"I'm sorry, but I've got to leave," she told Mark.

"Does duty call?"

"Yeah, pretty much."

An uneasy silence fell. Carly sensed that Mark wanted to know more about the case at hand, but of course Carly knew nothing about it herself, not yet.

Mark shrugged awkwardly.

"Well, I guess this is a pretty common thing for you, something that I …"

His voice trailed, but Carly knew what he was leaving unsaid. He'd have to get used to this kind thing if they ever got serious about each other—and that might not be easy for either one of them.

"I wish I could stay," Carly said.

"I understand. Good hunting."

"Thanks."

With a final glance at the slight grin on his handsome features, Carly hurried out of the restaurant and back toward her car.

CHAPTER FOUR

When Carly walked into Special Agent Voss's office, she was surprised to find him alone behind his desk.

Why isn't Lyle here yet? she wondered.

Her partner usually arrived first at the BAU Quantico headquarters. He lived nearby, and he'd told her on the phone he was more than eager to get going.

"I'm ready for another case. I'm gnashing at the bit."

Carly felt a sudden misgiving. Could Lyle be waiting in his own office for her to join him before they came to meet with Voss? She hadn't checked there or even gone to her own desk in the big general work area. When she'd gotten off the elevator and seen Voss's door standing open, she had assumed they were both waiting for her.

"Have a seat, Agent See," Voss said without rising.

She sat in one of the chairs in front of his desk. The team chief was large and stocky but not very tall. Years of office work had softened him around the middle, but he still retained the keen alertness of an active field agent.

Voss cradled his fingers together for a moment, as if trying to decide what he wanted to say. Finally he spoke in a worried tone she'd seldom heard from him before.

"I want to talk with you before Lyle joins us."

Carly was truly startled now. For one thing, Voss wasn't in the habit of referring to either Carly or her partner by their first names. Lyle and the Voss had known each other for years now—since before Voss had been put in charge. Even so, he always called them "Agent Ramsey" and "Agent See."

A short silence fell before Voss spoke again.

"I take it your partner's life was in danger during your last case."

"That's right, sir."

"And you saved his life?"

The question jarred Carly. She flashed back to the moment when she'd arrived at the scene just in time to find a psychopathic killer pointing Lyle's own gun at him while he lay paralyzed on the floor. She'd come very close to exchanging her own life for her partner's, but she'd been deterred by a mysterious voice.

"Don't do this, Carly."

It had been a woman's voice—that of some departed spirit. She'd warned Carly that what she was contemplating would kill Lyle with guilt. Then Carly had taken a split-second chance and saved Lyle's life without sacrificing her own. But she still didn't know who that spirit might have been.

In answer to the chief's question, Carly replied, "That often happens, sir. Lyle has done the same for me. More times than I've helped him out of trouble, I'm pretty sure."

"That's what partners do. But this time ..."

He fell silent for a moment again.

"I'm worried about him, Agent See. He called me earlier. He was anxious to get started on a new case. Too anxious, maybe. As you know, our physician strongly recommended he take some time off to rest. What's your assessment of his state of mind?"

"Sir, I'm not exactly comfortable about discussing this."

"I understand, and I respect that. Just tell me—do you think he's ready to start another case?"

Carly twisted uneasily in her chair before she answered.

"I suppose so—if *he* says he's ready. He knows more about himself than any doctor does. *Not* working could be more stressful than getting back on the job. A new case might be good therapy."

Or it might not be. Who am I to make that call?

A silence fell between Carly and the team chief.

Finally Voss said, "I hope it's understood that there are circumstances in which your loyalty to your partner must yield to other concerns. For example ... if Lyle started drinking again, I assume you'd report that."

A jolt passed through Carly's whole body. Her voice shook a little and she had to struggle not to sound defensive.

"He hasn't started drinking again."

At least not that I know of.

She was sure she'd recognize the signs of a relapse while she and Lyle were actively working on a case. But could she really vouch for the last few days, when they hadn't spent any time together?

"That wasn't exactly my question," Chief Voss said. "What I want to know is—given Agent Ramsey's history of alcohol abuse, would you report it to me if he did start drinking again?"

Carly suppressed a shudder.

"I'd have no choice, sir. It's my duty to report anything that might interfere with my partner's ability to do his job. The same goes for both of us. If my own abilities were—well, compromised, I believe he'd do the same. I'd count on it."

Voss's whole body seemed to relax a little. He picked up his cellphone and typed in a text. Carly guessed he was summoning Lyle to join them.

"I'm glad to hear that," the team chief told her. "And if I may let down my guard a little, I must admit that I'm asking as a friend as much as a superior. I've known Lyle for a long time. We've seen each other through some tough times, and we've both earned some gray hairs. I was there during his divorce, and when he was struggling to get sober, and also when his previous partner got killed. And he's been there for me through plenty of bad times."

Voss heaved a long, deep sigh.

"But I'm not his partner, and you are. These days you know Lyle better than anybody in the world. And I'm depending on you to look out for him."

"I promise to do that, sir."

At that moment, Carly's lanky African-American partner walked into the office. He was about to speak, but he turned to look at Carly with surprise.

He didn't expect me to already be here.

Worse, he surely must have realized that Carly and the chief had been talking alone together. And he was far too sharp not to have picked up on the subject of their conversation.

She couldn't help averting her eyes from his for a moment, and she was sure her face had reddened. Lyle stared at her for a couple of seconds, then his cheeks creased with a wide grin as he turned to Voss.

"I take it you've got a case for us, chief."

Chief Voss nodded.

"That I do, Agent Ramsey. The authorities in Harmonium, Pennsylvania, have asked for our help on what they think might to be a serial case, although they're not yet sure of it. It's an industrial town just this side of Pittsburgh on the Lenawha River. I can arrange a commercial flight for you to head out there right now."

"Naw, I'd rather drive," Lyle said with a scoff. "By the time we get on a plane, we could be most of the way there."

He turned to Carly.

"How about you, kid? With the leaves changing and all, it ought to be a beautiful drive."

He cracked his knuckles in what struck Carly as a somewhat forced show of enthusiasm.

But the drive might be good for both of us.

"Fine with me," she replied.

"OK, then," Voss said. "Have a seat, Agent Ramsey, and I'll tell both of you what I can about the case."

*

As Lyle headed the BAU-owned SUV from Quantico to Harmonium, Pennsylvania, he realized that his partner was being unusually quiet. Even though the view from Interstate 70 wasn't exactly scenic, he found it nice to have the windows rolled down so they could enjoy the warm autumn air. But he couldn't escape the feeling that all was not well between him and Carly.

In an effort to make conversation, he rolled up the windows and asked, "So what have you been doing with yourself during the last couple of days?"

Carly appeared to flinch a little.

"Oh, nothing much. Just trying to take care of a few odds and ends."

A few odds and ends? Lyle wondered.

There was obviously something Carly wasn't telling him.

Maybe more than one thing.

When he had walked into Chief Voss's office and found Carly already there, Lyle had noticed a palpable, telltale tension. He was sure he wasn't being paranoid in thinking they'd been talking about him. Chief Voss must have been trying to determine whether he was ready to start working on another case, despite a BAU physician's recommendation to the contrary. And their concern was only natural.

Even so, Lyle found it uncomfortable to have them talking behind his back. If they had doubts about his mental well-being, why couldn't they just ask him to his face?

Lyle stifled a sigh at the obvious answer to that question.

Because I'd lie to them, that's why.

If he told anyone the truth about how the New Mexico case had gotten under his skin, he'd probably be put on involuntary leave for quite some time. And he'd have to endure all sorts of counseling.

He felt his whole body react as he remembered the sting of the hypodermic needle in his shoulder, then the sensation of all his limbs turning to rubber as the paralytic drug took effect. He had collapsed to the floor and lost control of his weapon.

When Carly arrived at the scene, he'd been helpless as the killer tried to bargain with her.

"Drop your weapon and do everything I say. Then I'll let your friend go. It'll be your life for his."

Lyle had seen something awful in Carly's eyes at that moment.

She almost did it, he thought.

She almost sacrificed her own life for mine.

His paralysis had been so complete that barely a word could escape his lips.

He'd only felt that helpless once before, when his previous partner, Dawn Metcalf, lay bleeding to death at his feet. She'd stepped between Lyle and a shooter and had taken a bullet herself—whether accidentally or deliberately, Lyle couldn't hope to ever know.

And just days ago, Lyle had nearly lost Carly in much the same way. He couldn't bring himself to talk about his horrible spasm of sheer helplessness to Carly or Chief Voss or anyone else.

Nor could he tell anybody how desperately he wanted a drink …

Right now.

Right this minute.

But he was determined never to give in to that urge again.

So he'd equipped himself with an alternative. Stashed away in his go-bag was a bottle of lorazepam pills. Of course he hadn't been able to get the stuff with a prescription. No responsible doctor would have prescribed him a potentially addictive medication. Instead, he'd turned to one of his shadier connections from a past drug-related case—a pharmacy assistant with what might politely be called flexible ethics.

Lyle had used some of the pills during the last few days, enough to realize how easy it would be to become dependent on them. He knew he had to be careful with them. So he didn't plan on taking any of them while he was working on this case.

Even so, he was glad he'd brought them in his go-bag. No matter how strongly Carly, Voss, and especially the BAU physician would disapprove, it felt good to have the pills on hand as a safety net. Just knowing there was something he could take in place of alcohol might help him get through his spells of overwhelming anxiety.

He and Carly always had absolute respect for each other's privacy, so he was sure she wouldn't go through his go-bag and find the forbidden drug. Even so, he felt a pang of guilt for not telling her about the bottle outright. But if he did, he knew she'd have no choice but to call him out on it, perhaps even report it to Chief Voss.

Not an option.

Besides, it wasn't the only secret that existed between them. His partner had never explained her frequently uncanny hunches and intuitions. There were limits to honesty, after all, even between friends and partners.

What she doesn't know won't hurt her.

And besides, he reminded himself, *it's just a safety net.*

CHAPTER FIVE

"I don't like the looks of this town," Carly heard her partner mutter.

The town of Harmonium had just come into view across the Lenawha River. In the deepening gray twilight, Carly saw that the town appeared to be a jumble of dark buildings punctuated by weak spots of light.

I don't like the looks of it either, she thought as they took a bridge across the river.

A bad smell crept up from the water, prompting both of them to shut their windows. The bridge took them above the city's waterfront, where a mile or so of dimly-lit factory buildings stretched out below them.

The plant appeared to have been abandoned years ago, and the buildings looked desolate and empty. Then their route took them through Harmonium's downtown area, which looked all but dead, with little traffic, few pedestrians, and many boarded-up businesses.

"The mayor is waiting in his office for us," Lyle said. "You'd better call and let him know we'll be there in a few minutes."

Carly made the call and left the message with the mayor's secretary, who still happened to be in the office. Then Carly turned her thoughts to this already-offbeat assignment. It struck her as unusual that their first stop in Harmonium was going to be a visit to the mayor. Usually they began work by coordinating their own efforts with local law enforcement.

After all, she wondered, *how much can a mayor know about murders?*

But she'd actually spent much of the drive silently worried about Lyle. More than once she'd felt on the verge of clearing the air with him, telling him flat-out about Chief Voss's request that she report any serious changes in his behavior.

It's not like Lyle couldn't guess what we talked about.

In fact, that might be the reason he seemed so taciturn. But how could she openly broach the topic of whether he was at risk of drinking again? He'd been sober for years, since well before they'd started working together.

Maybe, she hoped, she wouldn't have to do that. If Lyle was in any trouble, getting back to work could be the only rehab he needed.

Meanwhile, the car wended its way up a steep hillside littered with small houses. Like the businesses downtown, many of them appeared unoccupied, and some of them were shuttered and decrepit.

"It looks like Harmonium is on its way to becoming a ghost town," Carly remarked after she finished her phone call.

"Sure does. My guess is that its factory got shut down years ago."

"Which means the town has been slowly dying ever since."

"Yeah, pretty much literally," Lyle said, pointing to a building they were passing. "I think that's the fifth funeral home I've seen since we drove into town. Death seems to be the only growing industry around here. Small wonder some maniac might find this a suitable locale for a few murders. Living here must be as depressing as hell."

They reached the crest of the ridge, where they arrived at Harmonium's City Hall, a two-story brick building with a clock tower and what must have once been a proud view over the city. They found that the building was still open, with a man on duty at a desk just inside. Direction signs showed that several of the town's municipal functions were headquartered here. In addition to the city council chamber and the mayor's office, the police department and courtroom were also listed.

"How convenient," Lyle remarked. "We should be able to get a lot done with one stop."

But the building was so quiet, Carly had to wonder if everybody they needed to see would still be at work.

They identified themselves to the man at the reception desk, who called the mayor's secretary to usher them through a silent hallway. The offices they passed appeared to be mostly closed for the night, but all the lights were on inside the mayor's darkly-paneled workplace. The mayor was a rotund and cheerful-looking man in his late fifties, wearing shirtsleeves and a vest. He stood up from his desk and walked over to greet them with handshakes.

"You're Agents See and Ramsey, I assume. I'm Ike Freelander, and I'm the mayor of Harmonium. Have a seat."

They all sat down, then Freelander leaned back in his chair and smiled.

"So, what do you think of our fair city so far?"

Carly and Lyle exchanged an awkward look. This seemed like a strange question to ask at the beginning of a murder investigation.

Carly hesitated to speak, but Lyle replied.

"It looks like it's seen better days."

Mayor Freelander's smile turned wistful.

"I appreciate your honesty, Agent Ramsey. In fact, I'd have been uneasy if you'd tried to sugarcoat it. We've got an urgent situation here in Harmonium, and I want to make sure you're serious about your job. Murder can get to be a numbing business over time, I'm sure. You can get jaded about your job."

Jaded? Carl thought.

That was an emotion she'd never felt as a BAU agent. And she didn't much like the mayor's insinuation.

"I think you should know," Freelander continued, "it was my idea to call for the FBI's help. The chief of police isn't wild about it. He's not even sure we're dealing with a serial killer, and in any case he'd prefer to solve this with his own people. But I don't want to take any chances."

He got up from his desk and opened the curtains behind it to reveal a panorama of the town below, including the abandoned factory.

"I grew up here. I can remember when this was a thriving, bustling mill town. The Bassman Industrial Manufacturing plant hired about a quarter of the population. This was a great place to live in those days, just full of movie theaters and department stores and family restaurants and excellent public schools."

He heaved a long, sad sigh as he looked out over the town.

"I also remember how broken my grandfather was when the plant closed down in the mid-70s, leaving the whole town high and dry. He'd been an electrical engineer at the Bassman plant all his adult life. He spent the rest of his years working as a janitor. I decided when I was still a kid …"

He paused again, as if choked with emotion.

"I decided I'd make Harmonium the kind of town my grandfather could be proud of if he came back. And I've been trying to do that all my life."

Pointing down at the factory, he added, "It may not look like it now, but we're rebuilding and revitalizing that whole area. When we get done, it'll be a bustling business and technology center. Harmonium will thrive just like it did in its heyday. But right now it's still touch and go—which is why I'm worried about these murders. Investors can get queasy over this kind of thing."

He sat back down again.

"So now you know," he said. "I'm really hoping you put your all into solving this case as quickly as possible."

Carly could practically feel Lyle bristle at this comment. For her part, she felt a pang of sympathy for the mayor's elegiac sentiments about Harmonium's past and his touching hopes for its future. If there really was a serial killer afoot in this town, the stakes were certainly very high.

Maybe the future of a whole town, she thought.

"I can assure you, my partner and I give our full attention to every case we work on," Lyle said. "We will do exactly the same here. With all due respect, your town's plans for the future won't affect our work one way or the other."

"Of course," Mayor Freelander said, his face reddening. He sounded embarrassed and maybe a little angry. "I apologize if I said anything out of line. Well, anyway, that's all I wanted to talk with you about. I'll have my secretary book you into a couple of rooms in the Cameron Hotel downtown for your stay here."

Rising from his desk, Freelander added, "You'll want to see our police chief, Vince Tallarico, right away. He can tell you everything you need to know. You'll find him at the other end of the complex."

As Carly and her partner followed the directional arrows through a series of hallways toward the police chief's office, Lyle growled resentfully.

"I shouldn't have snapped at him like that," he said. "It's just that I hate it when we have to deal with politicians at any level. I especially hate it when they imply that we might give less than a hundred percent unless they give us some kind of pep talk."

"I understand how you feel," Carly told him. "But it's never good to rile up the locals. Just try to stay cool, OK?"

Lyle let out a sour chuckle.

"It's a little late for that advice. Let's just hope the police chief isn't also into political fun-and-games."

Carly hoped so too.

She also hoped that Lyle's spells of prickliness weren't going to make their job harder.

CHAPTER SIX

"I take it you just got a talking-to from our mayor," Harmonium's Chief of Police Vincent Tallarico said as they all sat down in his office.

Carly guessed Tallarico —a short, muscular man with a buzzcut—to be perhaps a decade or so younger than the mayor. She appreciated that the chief got right to his point.

"He might have made it sound like I object to your presence here," Tallarico added. "That's not true, I'm always happy to get a bit of extra help. It's just that I think maybe calling in the FBI is a bit of overkill. Maybe more than a bit. I can't help thinking your time and talents would be better used elsewhere."

When neither Lyle nor Carly commented, Tallarico added, "But now that you're here, let's talk about the case. What did your superior at Quantico tell you about it?"

"Only what he knew," Lyle said. "It would help if you started telling us everything from scratch."

Tallarico nodded and brought up an assortment of official reports and crime scene photos on his computer screen. The first photos he showed them were of a raggedy, bearded dead man sitting upright against a wall, his body splattered all over with blood.

"Our first killing was a week ago," the chief told them. "A homeless man in his 50s. His body was found next to a drainage ditch under a bridge, reported by one of his homeless buddies. His throat was slit. You can see he was still holding a large pocket knife, so we'd thought it was a suicide—not an uncommon thing here in Harmonium, especially among the homeless population."

"What was his name?" Carly asked.

"His buddies just called him Slim. That's about all we know about him. No ID, and fingerprints didn't bring up any hits. Nobody was aware of any next of kin."

"What about the second victim?" Lyle asked.

Tallarico then showed some more photos revealing the corpse of a young woman lying in bed in a nightgown. She was drenched in blood.

"Her name was Sarah Tooley, and she was 27 years old. Her husband found her body like this when he got home from a night shift working as a maintenance man. She was killed three days ago."

"Why did it take until now to call us in?" Carly asked.

Tallarico grunted and shrugged slightly.

"Well, the truth was, we didn't even consider the possibility of a serial killer until this morning. There was no obvious connection between them. And I've still got my doubts about it. But let me show you something."

Tallarico pointed out two pictures that were blown-up details from the bedroom murder.

"You can see here that Sarah Tooley was holding a penny in her right hand. That seemed odd when we found her body, but we didn't give it any serious thought. But this morning one of our men who'd been at both murder scenes remembered something."

He showed another blown-up picture from the murder scene below the underpass.

"Here you can see a penny lying next to Slim's hand," Tallarico said.

"It looks like he dropped it when he died," Lyle commented.

"Yeah, maybe. But couldn't it be a coincidence?"

"I doubt it," Lyle replied.

"Anyway, you two are the behavioral analysis experts," Tallarico said. "Why would a serial killer leave pennies behind?"

Carly peered more closely at both photographs.

"Some serial killers like to leave calling cards, sort of like signatures. But a penny isn't much of a signature. It's small and subtle and easy to miss."

She paused and thought for a moment.

"It may have been something much more intimate and personal," she added. "A gesture of some kind. What kind of gesture, we don't know. And anyway, that's just a guess at this point. We still don't know for sure we're dealing with a serial killer."

Tallarico took a deep breath, then admitted, "Maybe it *is* a good thing you two are here. My people and I aren't used to dealing with whatever this is. I mean, with this kind of criminal psychology. And the sooner we can get this case out of the way, the better."

Tallarico turned away from the computer screen.

"So how do you want to get started?" he asked.

"First of all, forward all these files and photos to us," Lyle said. "Have you still got the victims' bodies in the morgue?"

"Not the homeless guy. But the last I heard, we've still got the woman's body in storage. Let's go pay a visit to our coroner. He's right next door."

Lyle and Carly followed Tallarico out of City Hall a short distance to a smaller building bearing the sign Lenawha County Coroner.

As they walked there, Carly realized she had something new to worry about. When viewing a murdered body, she often received messages from the victim. Those messages could be powerful and disorienting, and Carly sometimes found it hard to conceal her reactions.

The advice she'd given to Lyle a little while ago now seemed pertinent to herself.

Just try to stay cool.

They passed through the vestibule and into the morgue. There they found an aproned man hard at work over an open cadaver. It was far from the first time Carly had seen a corpse's exposed organs, but it was a sight she never quite got used to. It wasn't as though she found it shocking. But she couldn't help finding it unreal, as if the organs were made of plastic or some other synthetic material.

Tallarico spoke to the man, who had a ruddy complexion and unruly hair that he kept in place with a hairnet.

"Simon, you've got a couple of visitors."

The man put down his scalpel and stepped toward Carly.

"FBI agents, I hope," he said. "And not a moment too soon. I'm Dr. Simon Russo, the city coroner."

Carly and Lyle produced their badges and formally introduced themselves. Russo took off his bloodstained rubber gloves and shook hands with them.

"We understand that the body of the homeless man is no longer in storage," Lyle said to Russo.

"Well, we didn't know it might be a murder at the time," Russo said. "We always send unclaimed bodies off for storage at a facility just outside of town. If they aren't claimed in a few weeks, the bodies are cremated and buried in a field that's used for that purpose."

A regretful expression crossed his face.

"I must admit, I dropped the ball. When the man's body came in, and I saw the photos showing a knife in his hand, I jumped to the conclusion that he'd committed suicide. I put that in my official report, even after I examined the body. I should have been more diligent."

"What other conclusion could you have come to?" Tallarico asked.

"The right one, Vince. Let me show you."

Dr. Russo went to a file drawer and pulled out a folder and opened it to show some autopsy photographs of the corpse.

"Just this morning, when Vince stopped by to tell me we might be dealing with a serial killer, I took another look at these photos."

He showed the group a view of the open wound on the victim's neck.

"This wound was made by a blade that was thin and extremely sharp, with a sharp point—a box cutter or a utility knife of some sort, probably. There's no way he could have inflicted this wound on himself with that pocketknife of his. That would have been a whole lot messier."

"The crime scene photos actually suggested some kind of struggle," Tallarico admitted. "But I put that down to him thrashing around when he cut himself. Based on what you're telling me, the victim may have opened his pocketknife and tried to defend himself from whoever killed him. I should have seen that possibility."

"But the knife was bloody," Carly said, remembering the crime scene photos.

"Yeah, but so was everything else there," Tallarico said. "I'll put in an order for a forensic examination of the knife blade. If Simon is right, it will show that the knife wasn't used to cut anybody's flesh—or if it was, it would only have nicked the killer. There was no trail of blood to or from the crime scene."

Russo sighed bitterly.

"I guess there's a lesson to be learned here," he said. "Some people don't get their due from society. Homeless people, for example. And when they die, we brush it off; we don't pay enough attention. We don't ask the same questions. We don't give them their due respect. And I'm as guilty of that as anyone."

"Maybe I am too," Tallarico said with a nod of somber agreement.

While Carly was touched by the two men's regret, she thought there was another matter that they conspicuously didn't want to talk about. If they were, in fact, dealing with a serial killer, they might have stopped him from claiming a second victim if only they'd been more diligent about the homeless man.

There's no turning back the clock, Carly thought.

And we may be running way behind.

"Could we see the woman's body now?" Lyle asked.

"Of course," Russo said.

He escorted the group over to the wall stacked with steel storage drawers and opened one of them. Carly could see at a glance that the woman's corpse had been refrigerated for a while. There was a liquid pool under the corpse where the bodily fluids had largely passed through the skin, leaving the body itself looking parched and almost mummified.

The woman's mouth was hanging open—not in an expression of terror, Carly knew, but from the slackness that set in before the body had stiffened with rigor mortis.

"Let's have a look at this wound," Russo said.

Lyle and Tallarico stood beside him peering at the victim's neck.

Meanwhile, Carly was torn about what to do next. The surest way to get a message from the dead woman was to actually touch her body. But that had its risks. Was she ready to handle the onslaught of sensations that it might bring on? The last time she'd gotten a communication from a corpse in a morgue, the experience had knocked her nearly off her feet, causing alarm among the others present.

But if she wanted to do it, she had to do it now. The three men were attentively studying the wound and talking among themselves about it. Carly could actually touch the woman's thigh without them even noticing.

She reached cautiously toward the woman's flesh. But before her fingers made contact, she felt a sharp, painful charge, as if from an electrical shock. And she heard a voice call out inside her mind.

"Don't touch me!"

CHAPTER SEVEN

Carly snatched her fingers back to her side.

As startled as she felt, she hadn't lost control of the experience—at least not so far. She closed her eyes and focused on the spirit's presence. Again she heard a voice in her mind.

"How did you find me?"

"I'm here to help," Carly replied with her thoughts.

"What are you doing here?"

"I said I'm here to help."

Behind her closed eyelids, Carly found herself standing in a broad, dark, empty space with a large open box right in front of her.

"Go away," the voice said.

"But I'm here to help," Carly repeated.

"Go away, I said."

Carly realized the voice was coming out of the box. She stepped over to it and looked inside. Curled up tightly inside the box like a cat was the dead woman, wearing a bloody nightgown.

"Why are you hiding?" Carly asked.

"I'm in terrible danger," the woman said in a voice quavering with fear. *"You shouldn't be here. Go away. It's dangerous for you too. And don't tell anybody you saw me."*

Carly was puzzled.

Doesn't she know she's already dead?

Before Carly could say anything else, the sound of Lyle's voice yanked her out of the visitation.

"At least we know our killer isn't a sadist."

Carly's eyes snapped open, and she saw the three men studying the wound as before. Hardly any time had passed during her visitation, and none of her colleagues had noticed anything unusual about her behavior.

Chief Tallarico shook his head skeptically.

"Huh. He sure seems sadistic to me. He enjoys the sight of blood, anyway."

But Dr. Russo nodded in agreement with Lyle.

"I believe you're right, Agent Ramsey. The incision is so precise, the killer seems to be avoiding the infliction of gratuitous pain on his victims. He seems to have actually gone to some extra effort in that regard. And he was probably successful. Each of the victims felt a single swift, sharp cut, but then bled out quickly enough that they didn't suffer."

Dr. Russo shrugged and added, "In the case of the homeless man, a quick death like that might almost have been a blessing. Even though my autopsy on him wasn't as thorough as it should have been, it did show that he had a dangerously enlarged heart and a hopelessly damaged liver. He wouldn't have lived much longer, and his last days were sure to be hell for him. He suffered a lot less this way."

"But what about the woman?" Tallarico asked.

"That's a different story," Dr. Russo replied with a shrug. "She seemed to be perfectly healthy."

"That's what her husband told me," Tallarico said.

Carly and Lyle exchanged glances at the mention of the victim's husband. Simply as a matter of procedure, a victim's spouse was automatically a person of interest, at the very least.

"I take it you've already interviewed the victim's husband," Lyle remarked to Tallarico.

"Yeah, and he's in the clear. He was at work that day."

Carly said, "But I don't suppose you've talked to him since you realized you might be dealing with a serial killer."

"No, but what difference would that make?"

Maybe a lot, Carly thought. She wondered how carefully that alibi had been checked out. In any case, the situation had changed, and there were plenty of new questions to ask.

Lyle thanked Dr. Russo for his help and stepped out of the morgue. As Carly and Tallarico followed him into the hallway, she noticed the Police Chief glancing at his watch. She thought that Tallarico looked impatient as Lyle came to a halt and turned to speak to them.

"I think we need to talk to the woman's husband," Lyle told the chief.

"Now might not be the best time. Like I said, he works a night shift—midnight to eight. He's likely to be fast asleep right now. Maybe we should call ahead."

"And maybe we shouldn't," Lyle said. "Sometimes courtesy isn't the best approach. If there's any chance he's our killer, we don't want to give him a heads up."

"Suit yourself. But I really don't think he's our man."

"Duly noted. Just remember—this is an FBI case now."

"Fine," Tallarico grumbled. "You call the shots."

The chief looked at his watch again.

"But I'm afraid I can't join you to interview the husband if you want to do it right now. I've got an important appointment coming up."

More important than a possible serial case? Carly wondered.

"Not a problem," Lyle replied amiably. "We'll keep you in the loop."

Looking relieved, Tallarico handed them the case folders.

"You'll find everything you need to know here, including the victim's address. For the record, though, I'm still not convinced we're dealing with a serial. Despite that, I get that you're in charge, and I'm OK with it. But show some finesse while you're here. Don't make a mess of things. And don't go showboating or making a big display of yourselves. The mayor has his own reasons for wanting to wrap this up quickly and quietly. And I've got my reasons, too."

With that, Tallarico hurried away down the hall.

The chief's words rattled through Carly's head as and she and Lyle walked outside toward their vehicle.

"So what do you think about the case?" Carly asked Lyle.

"My gut tells me that we're dealing with a real serial killer. I just wish Chief Tallarico was on the same page."

"What do you make of him?"

"Why? Do you think he's mysterious or something?"

"Well, something seems wrong about him to me. I'd have thought he'd be eager to come with us to talk to the husband."

"I'm just as glad he didn't. Wouldn't you rather do an interview without the locals hovering over you?"

"Sure, but didn't he actually kind of blow us off? And why is he so worried that we'll 'make a mess of things?'"

Lyle's cheeks creased as he grinned.

"Well, I'm surprised you don't have him all figured out by now. Like the mayor, he's lived in this town all his life. But he's too young to remember what Harmonium was like in its heyday, so he doesn't have the mayor's sentimental feelings about it. Do you follow me so far?"

"I guess."

Carly suppressed a giggle. Although she hadn't thought of that before, her partner's deductions about the chief struck her as right on. Most of all, she was relieved to hear him sounding like his old self-confident self.

"The Police Chief has hated this town all his life," Lyle continued. "He probably got married too young and started having kids too early, so he got stuck in this town whether he wanted to or not. But now his kids are grown, and he may or may not be divorced, and he wants to pull up roots and plant them elsewhere."

"You mean he's looking for another job."

"Exactly. And as far away as he can get from Harmonium. His biggest fear is of rotting away here in his old age. What do you think that 'appointment' of his is all about? He's got a conference call or a video conference set up to interview for a job. He doesn't want to bother himself any more with serial killer business. He'd just like it to go away. But he's kind of in a bind. 'Don't go showboating,' he said. He doesn't want us to hurt his job prospects by making him look bad. If this is a real serial case, he doesn't like the idea of us getting too much of the glory."

Lyle chuckled heartily

"So does he still seem mysterious to you?"

"I guess not."

In fact, everything Lyle had just said made perfect sense to Carly. This was exactly the kind of thinking he was good at—and his profiling skills often yielded clearer insights than her own secret contacts with the dead. Her visions and hearing voices were often riddling and sometimes incomprehensible. The dead weren't always lucid, and it often wasn't clear how much they actually knew about their own circumstances.

And yet she knew that their communications gave her information they could never get anywhere else.

Whenever I can figure out what those messages mean.

As Lyle drove through the city streets, Carly kept thinking about her vision of the terrified dead woman lying curled up in that box.

Sarah Tooley might not even know she's dead yet.

"I'm in terrible danger," the frightened spirit had said.

But what kind of danger could a murdered spirit possibly fear?

And why had the spirit also warned, *"It's dangerous for you too."*

CHAPTER EIGHT

"First," Lyle commented as they approached the old apartment building. "How do you suppose the killer got in?"

The glass doors to the building looked pretty secure to Carly. She and Lyle had both gone over the police reports after he drove them here, but they'd found no assumption about that question.

"Maybe he lived here," she said.

"Possibly. But the local cops checked out the residents and didn't come up with anything. According to the report, the back delivery door is even tighter than this one."

On the wall beside the entry was a large panel of buzzers and a metal grill covering a mic, so visitors could ask a specific tenant to trip the lock so the door would open.

"Well, we can be pretty sure the victim didn't buzz him in," Carly said. "She seems to have been asleep in bed at the time of the attack. He took her by surprise. My guess is she didn't know him."

"Unless the killer was her husband."

"Chief Tallarico said he has an alibi."

"Uh-huh."

Carly wasn't surprised that her partner was also skeptical about that alibi.

She stepped back and looked up at the shabby-looking building. It had once looked modern, with rows of balconies overlooking a rather unattractive neighborhood. But those balconies were too high for anyone to reach without elaborate equipment. Maybe the man who had terrified and murdered Sarah Tooley either had a key or faked his way in via the buzzer system. Sometimes a tenant in this kind of place might fall for a counterfeit delivery man or some other plea for entry.

But would that be likely in the middle of the night? she wondered.

She reached for the button to the dead woman's apartment. The husband was supposed to be at home, so maybe they could get him to buzz them in.

At that moment a man appeared inside the front foyer and pushed his way out through the glass door, seemingly oblivious to any other presence there. The door swung back slowly as the man walked away, giving anyone plenty of time to duck inside before it closed again.

Carly took advantage of the chance to hold the door open.

"Hey!" Lyle called out to the man who was leaving.

The man turned and looked back at him from the sidewalk. Lyle produced his badge.

"I'm Special Agent Lyle Ramsey with the FBI, and this is my partner, Agent See."

"So?"

"So, you just left this door wide open for us to walk right inside."

"OK," the man replied with a shrug. "You're welcome."

"Are you aware that a murder took place in this building three days ago?"

"Yeah, I heard something about that. It's got nothing to do with me. I don't even live on the floor where it happened."

Carly could see that Lyle was getting a bit annoyed.

"You've got a security buzzer out here for a reason," Lyle explained. "You just left the door standing so we could walk right in. We could have been anybody."

"But you're actually FBI."

"That's not the point."

The man looked as though he sincerely didn't understand the problem.

"Are you going to arrest me?" he asked.

"No."

"OK, then. It's a free country. Like I said, you're welcome."

The man walked away, whistling along the street.

"The security for this building is like a sieve," Lyle grumbled. "All someone would have to do to get in here is wait for someone else to open the door. And take a look at that."

As he and Carly walked into the little foyer, Lyle pointed to a security camera that was hanging loose from its cable, obviously broken.

"I doubt the killer did that," Carly said.

"No. It's probably been broken for a long time."

"Well, at least the husband won't be expecting us. That might work to our advantage."

A sign on the elevator in the foyer read OUT OF ORDER. They headed to a stairwell and climbed three flights up to the floor where the victim had lived.

When they stepped into the hallway, Carly was struck by the smell of mildew and cooking and unidentified odors. Music ranging from pop to Heavy Metal blared from the surrounding apartments. As they made their way to the victim's apartment, they heard shouting from the one next door. A man and woman were trading curses, and a baby was screaming.

"I'd sure hate to live in this place," Lyle said, raising his voice to be heard over noise.

"I would too."

When they stopped in front of the door they were looking for, Lyle commented, "This one wouldn't have stopped anybody who knew what he was doing."

"I see that. Anyone with a lock pick set could get in here in a matter of seconds. Either one of us could do it."

"And this place is probably noisy at night too. So the victim wouldn't necessarily hear him coming, especially if she was sleeping."

"So maybe it wasn't the husband after all."

Lyle knocked sharply on the apartment door.

"Who is it?" a man's voice called from inside.

"FBI," Lyle said. "We want to come in and talk."

There was no reply for a few moments.

"I talked to the police already," the man finally said.

"I know. But we've got a few more questions."

More seconds passed. Then the door opened, revealing a muscular young man of medium build wearing jeans and a t-shirt.

"Come on in," he said.

Carly and Lyle entered a small, shoddy room with a sliding door that opened out onto the little balcony. All of the furniture looked old and worn.

"I take it you're Scott Tooley," Lyle said.

The man nodded curtly.

Lyle produced his badge and introduced himself and Carly.

"We're here to talk about the murder of your wife," he said.

"We're sorry for your loss," Carly added.

"Thanks," Tooley replied. "Have a seat."

Lyle and Carly sat down on the couch and took out their notebooks, but Tooley remained conspicuously on his feet, striding back and forth with a dull, blank look on his face. Carly could see that the out-of-date shag carpet was matted down where he was walking.

This guy has been doing a lot of pacing, she thought. *And he hasn't been getting a lot of sleep. Is he feeling guilty?*

Lyle began the interview.

"Mr. Tooley, I'm sorry if we have to ask you questions you've answered before, but please bear with us. Do you know anyone who might have meant your wife any harm?"

"No. No one. Everybody liked her. At her job too."

Carly and Lyle exchanged a glance at this predictable answer.

Now for the sensitive question.

"Mr. Tooley, how have things been between you and Sarah recently?" she said.

"Good."

Carly and Lyle exchanged another glance at this monosyllabic reply.

"What about tension between the two of you?"

Tooley shifted his weight uneasily but didn't reply.

"It wouldn't be all that unusual," she said gently. "It's just that we really need to know everything about the situation."

"OK, things weren't perfect. We were working separate hours, and we weren't seeing much of each other, and we sometimes argued."

"Did that ever lead to physical violence?" Lyle asked.

"No. God no. The truth is, we were both awfully tired. She was putting in long days as a gift shop clerk, and I've been working nights as a janitor."

Carly noted his distaste when he said the word "janitor." Had Sarah shared that feeling? Did this man feel guilty about not being more of a provider? Of course, Sarah's job as a cashier hadn't been exactly glamorous either.

But his job left his wife alone at night, Carly thought.

She sensed that Tooley was haunted by guilt, but it was over not being here to protect Sarah.

"Did either of you ever have children?" she asked.

Tooley shook his head no.

"Were children in your plans?" Lyle put in.

"We talked about it. That's all we ever did, though. We talked about it."

He said those last words in a bitter monotone, almost as if he were reading them off a page. Then he made eye contact for the first time—first with Lyle, and then with Carly.

"Look, I don't want to tell you how to do your job, but I didn't kill my wife. I was working at the time. My company has records to prove it. And whoever killed her is still out there. Shouldn't you be looking for him?"

"We've got to do certain things by the book, Mr. Tooley," Lyle said. "Just bear with us, please."

Carly knew it wasn't necessarily the answers to their stock questions that might tip them off to a killer. *How* the possible suspect answered those questions might matter more—the words he chose, his body language, his apparent evasions.

She also knew that the living environment might harbor clues of its own. As she looked around the room, she was struck by a number of framed photographs hanging on the walls. They were mostly melancholy images, like empty houses and closed-up businesses and buildings in the ruined factory

"Did you take these photographs?" she asked Tooley.

"No, that was Sarah. They're all places around Harmonium. How it is here these days."

"They're quite good," Carly said. "Did she ever think about becoming a professional photographer?"

"No, it didn't seem to occur to her. At least, she never said anything. Maybe I should have … encouraged her."

The regret in his voice was palpable.

Another thing he feels guilty about.

Carly knew that grief from personal experience. After her sister disappeared, she'd also regretted missed moments for kindness and nurturing.

Scott was going to be dealing with these emotions for a long time.

She turned her attention toward a closed door.

"Is that the bedroom … where it happened?" she asked.

Tooley nodded mutely.

"May I go in and have a look?"

Tooley shrugged.

"Go ahead. There's not much to see, though. I … cleaned everything up. The cops said it would be OK."

Lyle took over the questioning then, so Carly got up quietly and opened the bedroom door. The room was tiny, with more framed photographs all over the walls. Most of the space was taken up by a queen-size bed.

There was still a broad red bloodstain in the carpet. Even with his janitorial skills, and probably with the help of industrial strength detergents and disinfectants, Tooley hadn't been able to get rid of it.

No one ever will, Carly realized.

The carpet was going to have to be completely replaced. Carly paused to wonder. if Tooley moved out, would he lose his rent deposit over that?

Sort of a cynical question.

But nothing about this building suggested to her that the owner was especially sensitive about such matters.

By contrast, the bed was immaculately made, with a clean blanket and fluffed-up pillows. Of course the mattress underneath must be caked thick with dried blood.

Carly felt sure that Tooley hadn't slept there since the murder. He had carefully remade the bed and hadn't touched it since. Perhaps he'd slept on the couch where Lyle was now sitting, but somehow she even doubted that.

He's barely slept at all.

Nothing about Scott Tooley's behavior suggested to Carly that he was his wife's killer. But she warned herself not to jump to conclusions.

Through the narrowly open door, Carly could hear Lyle still asking routine questions. Tooley's answers remained spare and simple, at least when he knew the answers at all.

Standing in the bedroom, Carly found herself thinking about the brief, puzzling communication back at the morgue.

"I'm in terrible danger," the voice had said, as if the victim wasn't aware that her murder had already happened.

Carly shivered.

If she touched that bed she might—just might—get another communication. And this time she had a moment to herself, so she wouldn't have to hide her reactions. If the spirit could give her a clearer message, she didn't dare miss the opportunity.

Cautiously, she reached forward and laid her hand on the blanket.

The effect was powerful and instantaneous.

CHAPTER NINE

The shock ran through Carly's body like electricity. She saw that her hand was now touching a coffin made from dark varnished wood with shiny brass bars along its sides. The bed, the bedroom itself, had been replaced by a vision.

But as she stood there, she didn't hear any sort of message. She didn't even feel the presence of a spirit.

She wondered briefly what to do next. Unlike other visitations from the dead, this time it seemed to be up to her to start the conversation.

Finally she closed her fist and knocked softly on the coffin lid.

"Who are you?" a faint voice murmured from inside.

Carly replied silently with her thoughts.

"You spoke to me earlier."

She heard a deep sigh from within the coffin.

"Didn't I tell you to stay away?"

"All I want to do is help."

"You can't help, you foolish woman. I'm dead. I'm beyond help."

Carly paused for a moment. The spirit seemed to have a clearer idea of her situation than before. At least, she knew that she was dead.

And, whether she realized it or not, this spirit had reached out to her.

"I want to find who did this to you," Carly said with her thoughts.

"What does it matter now?"

"Because he already killed someone else before he killed you. And he's going to kill again."

"We all wind up here sooner or later."

"But that's not the point."

"There is no point. You don't belong here. I do. Soon I'll be with Amber. She's waiting for me."

"But—"

"Don't you see where you are?" the spirit interrupted. *"Just look around. You don't belong here. Not yet."*

Carly stared at the coffin for a moment. Then she became aware of something in the air. It was a cold, salty dampness blowing through her hair and against her cheeks. Even over the rumble of a powerful engine, she could hear the cries of seagulls in the wind.

She wondered—was she back on the boat to Santa Novara again?

No, that can't be.

She stepped back and looked around.

The coffin she had been touching was at the bottom edge of a hundred or more that were neatly stacked in the shape of a pyramid. That pyramid of coffins was on a large, flat-bottomed boat moving over a seemingly endless sea. Enormous seagulls were diving down around her.

It's a ferryboat, she realized.

But instead of being loaded with vehicles, it was loaded with coffins. And as she looked out over the water, she saw headstones rising up among the waves. Soon the whole sea appeared to be full of them.

Carly turned back to the coffins, hoping to talk with the spirit again. But she couldn't hold onto the vision. As it faded away, she realized that she was standing in the bedroom with her eyes closed. She could hear Lyle's voice from the adjoining room.

"Mr. Tooley, perhaps you aren't aware of this, but we believe a serial killer might be at large."

Carly opened her eyes. Although she could see her normal surroundings now, her mind was reeling from one of the strangest visions she'd ever experienced.

What could it mean? she wondered.

Lyle's voice continued, "And we believe your wife was his second victim."

Then a silence fell.

Carly forced herself to concentrate on the present. She knew that Lyle had timed this crucial remark to best gauge Tooley's reaction to it. She stepped out of the bedroom to see his reaction for herself.

For the first time, Tooley appeared to be shaky on his feet. He tottered a bit, then sat down in an upholstered armchair.

"My God," he said with a shake of his head. "This can't be real."

He fell silent, and Carly and Lyle both let the silence linger as they tried to read his expression. His gaze had turned inward, and he'd become markedly paler. It was the sort of stupefied reaction that Carly knew was very difficult to fake. And of course, Lyle knew it too.

But don't jump to conclusions.

Tooley's eyes darted between Carly and Lyle and he sputtered desperately.

"Do you really think I … ? Am I a suspect or … ? Are you going to arrest me or … ? Should I call a lawyer or …? What's going on here, anyhow?"

"Relax," Lyle said. "We're not arresting you. All we want right now is your full cooperation. Take a few deep breaths."

Carly knew that her partner was allowing Tooley a moment to gather his wits before pushing him any further. She caught Lyle's look and nod, which she knew was a signal for her to finish up the interview. She was certain that the spirit who contacted her was this man's murdered wife, and she remembered the name that spirit had mentioned with a note of grief in her voice.

"Soon I'll be with Amber. She's waiting for me."

Slowly and carefully, Carly began to broach the subject.

"Mr. Tooley … was your wife depressed lately?"

Tooley squinted at her curiously.

"What's that got to do with anything? Are you suggesting she committed suicide? Because just now your partner said she was killed by a serial killer."

"I'm not suggesting anything like that," Carly said gently. "But Sarah's emotional state might be important. Please tell me."

"She was … sad lately," Tooley said.

"Why?"

"A childhood friend of hers died from leukemia about a month ago."

"What was her name?" Carly asked—although she was pretty sure she already knew the answer.

"Amber Jordan. Sarah took it very hard. She wished she could have spent more time with her friend in the hospital during her last days, but that was hard because of her work schedule, and Sarah felt very guilty about it. She had a hard time getting over it."

Tooley shook his head and added, "To tell the truth, I was worried about Sarah. But what does this have to do with her murder?"

Maybe nothing, Carly thought.

But the name did support the authenticity of her odd visionary experience. At times, Carly couldn't be positive whether her hallucinations were real visitations or figments of her imagination or some combination of both. This one had been real.

But was it going to be of any help to the investigation? Coffins loaded onto a modern-day ferryboat sailing a vast sea that sprouted tombstones seemed weirdly symbolic, but how could she hope to make sense of it?

As if looking for an answer to that question, Carly glanced around the room. Her eyes fell upon the small group of photos hanging on a nearby wall.

The photos were of a cemetery. One of them showed a statue of an angel with outstretched wings, her head buried in her hands. The other pictures were shot so that the rows of tombstones seemed to go on endlessly toward some unseen horizon.

Carly felt a tingle of realization.

A sea of gravestones.

Was the sea in her dream symbolic of a cemetery?

She pointed to the photos and said, "Mr. Tooley, where did your wife shoot those photos?"

"Over at Westcliff Cemetery. Why?"

"They're intriguing images. Did Sarah have … any personal connection with that cemetery?"

Tooley's eyes widened with surprise.

"It's weird that you'd ask," he said. "Her cousin, Lon Foster, works there. He's the groundskeeper. It's an old cemetery and full of statues and stuff like that. He told her maybe she'd like to take pictures there, so she did."

Carly was aware that Lyle was staring at her curiously. Of course he had no idea why she had started into this line of questions.

"What can you tell me about her cousin?" Carly asked Tooley.

Tooley shuddered.

"The best I can say about him is that Sarah always tried to think the best of him. He's not a good guy. He's gotten arrested for assault several times, and he served 18 months at the penitentiary in Greensburg for dealing heroin. He's been out on parole for several months. I kept telling Sarah she ought to stay away from him, but she really wanted to help him get a fresh start in life."

Tooley leaned in his chair toward Carly.

"Do you think he might have … ?"

"I don't know. You know him better than I do. What do you think?"

Tooley shuddered again and shook his head.

"I don't know what to think. About anything. All I can say is that I worried about Sarah every time she went near that guy. But she had a kind heart. Maybe it was too kind for her own good."

A silence fell.

"Mr. Tooley, could you tell us where we could find Lon Foster?"

"Sure. He's a live-in groundskeeper right there at that cemetery. He's got his own little house next to the main offices."

Tooley then gave them directions.

"Thanks for your time and help, Mr. Tooley," Carly said. "And again, we're very sorry for your loss."

Lyle added, "I suppose it goes without saying that you shouldn't leave Harmonium during the next few days. We may need to ask more questions. Also, get in touch if anything pertinent occurs to you."

"I'll do anything to help," Tooley replied. "Just catch whoever did this to Sarah, OK?"

"We'll do our best," Carly told him.

When Carly and Lyle headed out of the apartment, the hallway was still noisy. The couple next door seemed to have stopped arguing, but their baby was still crying and rowdy music blasted behind some other walls. Lyle was silent as they continued on their way out of the building, but Carly knew his mind was full of unanswered questions.

As they walked away from the building, she felt a smattering of raindrops. By the time they got into their vehicle, a light drizzle was falling. Without a word, Lyle started the engine and started to drive, following the directions to Westcliff Cemetery.

"What do you think of Scott Tooley?" he finally asked.

"I don't think he's the killer."

"No, I don't suppose I do, either. It's too soon to rule him out, though."

Lyle seemed to hesitate, then said, "Would you mind telling me why we're on our way to visit the victim's cousin?"

"You don't think he sounds suspicious?"

"I suppose so, maybe. But probably no more so than lots of other people in this town. The homeless man wasn't anywhere near here when he was killed."

"That doesn't mean there isn't a link."

"No, but don't you think it's kind of a leap to assume there *is* a connection? I mean, without even checking back through Chief Tallarico's research so far? We should try to find something to back us up. Maybe we can follow up on this tomorrow."

Carly fell silent. Lyle sounded tired and irritable, and it was rather late in the day now. Darkness and falling rain didn't make the idea of visiting a graveyard appealing. But when they were on an investigation, Lyle was usually the last one to call it quits for the day. She had to wonder if his stamina was still affected by his awful experience in New

Mexico.

"It's just a hunch," she finally said.

Lyle let out a discontented growl.

"Well, I know better than to ignore your hunches. They often pan out. But one of these days …"

His voice faced, but Carly knew what he was leaving unsaid.

"One of these days you're going to have to explain these hunches of yours."

It was true, of course. And Carly sensed that "one of these days" was coming up sooner rather than later. But would Lyle believe her, or would he think she was crazy?

CHAPTER TEN

"A sea of gravestones," Carly muttered.

"What?" Lyle asked. He was driving their vehicle on the curved road that led into Westcliff Cemetery. Even through the rain-streaked car windows Carly could see hundreds of gravestones flanking the road.

She hadn't realized she'd spoken aloud, but she wasn't ready to tell Lyle about her vision of gravestones in an open sea.

And here was something very much like it in real life.

"It's like a sea out there," she replied.

"Just a little shower. I think the rain is actually letting up now."

Lyle drove to the stone building where the main offices were located. Of course the place was closed up for the night. But just as Scott Tooley had told them, there was a brick cottage near the main building.

"That must be it," Carly said. "Where the groundskeeper lives."

"We might need our flashlights."

"And ponchos."

They pulled on their ponchos and got out of the car. The area was dimly lit, but there were no outside lights at all farther away from these buildings and the road. A glow from the cottage windows indicated that someone was probably at home.

Lyle knocked on the door sharply.

"Who is it?" a man's voice called out.

"Is this Lon Foster?" Lyle called back.

"Who wants to know?"

"FBI agents," Lyle said. "We just want to come in and talk."

Carly heard indistinct cursing from inside, then some shuffling and clattering from deep inside the little building.

"He's going to run," Lyle grumbled. "Be ready to call it in."

He switched on his flashlight and headed around the side of the house.

Carly took out her cellphone, but before she could make a call, she heard her partner shout.

"Stop!"

A hooded figure darted past the house toward the cemetery

Lyle was close behind.

Carly herself was in motion as she called the police switchboard.

"This is FBI Agent See. We've got a Code 2 at Westcliff Cemetery—a runner. Send backup. No deadly force necessary."

At least I hope not, she thought.

She quickened her pace to a trot and switched on her flashlight. For a moment the beam glittered off of raindrops and she couldn't see much else. Then her vision adjusted as her flashlight began to pick out the gravestones. Lyle's flashlight beam was darting like a firefly through the darkness some distance away.

He must be on the runner's trail.

But then that flashlight beam became stationary. Her partner had stopped running. He must have lost track of the fleeing man.

Carly stood still. It seemed likely that Foster might be hiding somewhere on the grounds. Everything here must be familiar to him, but she and Lyle could only creep around with their flashlights hoping to flush him out. Fortunately the rain was lighter now, but even so, the darkness around her seemed impenetrable beyond a few feet.

She heard Lyle's voice, and it sounded like he was moving farther away

"Like I told you Foster, we just want to ask a few questions. We're not here to make trouble."

There was no reply.

Standing alone in the dark and the drizzling rain, Carly turned in a circle, shining her light around to help get her bearings. She thought Foster had probably run off in some other direction, but it was also possible that he had doubled back toward her.

She felt a sudden jolt as her beam fell on a tall, pale human figure.

Then she saw that the figure's head was buried in its hands and it had wings outstretched at its back. She remembered it from one of the Sarah Tooley's photographs—a marble angel here to mark a grave.

Don't let this place get to you.

She made her way carefully along, using her light to check behind the larger headstones. Some of them were ornately curved and others were tall solid rectangles. A few were adorned with images of angels or other weeping figures. But she saw no one hiding, and she heard no one running.

Then Carly stumbled and almost tripped over a metallic object on the ground. In her flashlight beam, she saw what appeared to be a small tin fishing tackle box.

As she picked up the box, she heard a sound from somewhere off in the dark. She whirled around to see a flashlight approaching through the rows of headstones.

That sound was sloshing footsteps coming toward her.

She breathed a sigh of relief when she heard Lyle's voice.

"I've got him."

Her partner was shoving the runner ahead of him. Lon Foster's hands were cuffed behind him, and he was peering at Carly in the dim light. The man was short, muscular, and hulking, and his brow jutted over his eyes.

"This guy won't listen to me," the handcuffed man complained. "He's making a big mistake."

"I think you're Lon Foster." Lyle said, giving him a forward push. "Am I mistaken?"

"Maybe I am, and maybe I'm not."

"I'll take that as a yes. Mind telling us why you ran?"

"Bad times with cops. And you said FBI. What does the FBI want with me? I don't get it."

When Carly held the metal box up into the light, the captive gasped and cursed.

"Something in that box you don't want us to see?" Lyle asked.

"That isn't mine. I don't know where it came from."

Then came the sound of approaching sirens.

"You don't, huh?" Lyle said with a chuckle. "Well, I'm curious about what's inside. Let's get indoors where it's dry and have a look."

By the time Carly, Lyle, and the handcuffed man got back to the cottage, a couple of curious-looking cops had arrived carrying big flashlights. They all went inside the cottage, which was warm and dry. It might have been a cozy place except for the trash and dirty dishes and general disarray.

Lyle shoved the rain-drenched runner into a chair. Then he joined Carly and the other two cops to see what was in the little tin box.

Carly had pretty good idea what the contents must be. She remembered what Scott Tooley had said about Sarah's cousin—that he was out on parole after serving 18 months for dealing heroin. Foster must have rushed out of the house with the box, hoping to drop it somewhere out of sight. And he might have succeeded if Carly hadn't accidentally stumbled over it.

Sure enough, the lid snapped open to reveal a neat array of small plastic bags containing some sort of white powder.

"Looks like you're back in business, Lon," Lyle said with a chuckle. "Too bad about what this means for your parole, though."

"That's not mine," Foster complained loudly. "I swear it. I've got no idea where it came from."

Lyle patted Foster on the shoulder.

"I'm sure it's just a misunderstanding. And I'm sure we won't find your fingerprints on any of this stuff. No forensic evidence of any kind. I'll tell you what—let's take you somewhere where you can get dry, and you can clear everything up there once you're nice and toasty. But before we go …"

Leaning forward, Lyle towered over him.

"Could you tell me where you were and what you were doing in the small hours of the morning, three nights ago?"

"Huh?"

"I think you heard me."

"I—I don't understand. What do you think I … ?"

Foster's voice faded. Then his eyes widened. Carly could see that his brain was clicking away with a terrible realization.

"Is this about what happened to … ?"

His voice faded again before he could say his cousin's name.

Then he shook his head vigorously.

"No. No. You've got this wrong. I didn't … I would never …"

"You'd never what?" Lyle asked.

Foster fell silent for a moment.

"I'm not saying anything else without a lawyer."

"That can be arranged," Lyle replied. Then he told the cops, "Put this guy under arrest. He eluded us and evaded apprehension. More to the point, we caught him with a tin box full of illegal drugs."

Lon Foster just said one word.

"Lawyer."

Then two cops led him away.

When Lyle and Carly got back into their own vehicle, Lyle seemed to deflate like a punctured balloon.

"Damn it. What a waste of time."

"We made an arrest."

"Yeah, but do you really, seriously think Foster is our killer?"

The question brought Carly up short. In all the excitement of the last few minutes, she'd not really had a chance to consider the man's guilt one way or the other.

She said, “First thing tomorrow morning we can interrogate him and …”

Lyle interrupted sharply.

“And what? He’ll cave in and confess to two murders? I doubt that very much. Be honest with me, Carly. Be honest with yourself. What does your gut tell you about this guy?”

Carly swallowed hard. Now that she had a moment to think about it, she found it hard to believe Foster ever murdered anybody.

But it’s not impossible, she reminded herself.

Lyle stared through the windshield at the falling rain.

“Never mind,” he finally growled, starting the car engine, and turning on the headlights. “It was a good night’s work, doing the local cops’ job for them, getting Harmonium’s drug dealers off the street. Tallarico will be grateful. And I’m sure Chief Voss will be proud of us when we file our report. I’m sure he’ll overlook how we failed to catch a serial killer.”

Carly’s eyes widened with alarm.

We haven’t failed at anything, she wanted to say.

But she had to admit to herself there were a lot of things they didn’t know. Aside from not knowing for sure whether Lon Foster was a serial killer, they didn’t even know for absolute certain that there even *was* a serial killer.

Anyway, it would be very unusual for them to crack a murder case during their first day on the job. There would be more work to do tomorrow.

“Just give me directions to the place where the mayor made reservations for us,” Lyle said as they pulled out of the cemetery parking lot. “The Cameron Hotel. I hope they’ve held our rooms.”

Carly brought up the GPS directions and read them to Lyle as they drove through the desolate, rainy streets of Harmonium. She soon realized that her partner was looking grim as he stared out through the windshield.

“Lyle, do we need to clear the air about anything?” she finally said.

Lyle scoffed irritably.

“Yeah, maybe we do. Maybe you can tell me why you sent us chasing down some drug dealer when we need to stop a murderer from killing again. I trust your instincts, I really do, but honest to God, sometimes I wonder …”

His voice faded for a moment, then he spoke again through clenched teeth.

"Can you just tell me *why?"*

Carly shuddered. How could she begin to tell him about her contact with the dead woman and her vision of an ocean of gravestones? The possibility that her vision had led them up a blind alley made that all the more impossible.

"I just had a hunch," she said in a hushed voice.

"A hunch. Yeah. You get those a lot."

And that was the question that stood between them: her strange hunches and where they came from. She couldn't blame him for being puzzled, but she didn't think this was the time to try to explain herself. Not when they were both wet and exhausted. And especially not since Lyle seemed to be unusually irritable lately.

Carly and her partner had ordinary arguments in the past, but she was afraid that this one might spin out of control.

The Cameron Hotel was a shabby-looking brick building flanked by boarded-up businesses and a parking lot. Lyle parked in the lot, turned off the engine, and put on his poncho and grabbed his go-bag.

"Get a good night's sleep," Lyle said tersely. "Tomorrow's going to be a long day."

Without waiting for her to join him, Lyle got out of the car and stalked toward the front entrance.

Is Lyle close to a breaking point? Carly wondered.

If so, what was she going to do about it?

She put on her own poncho and picked up her go-bag and trudged tiredly through the wet night to the old hotel.

CHAPTER ELEVEN

Lyle stumbled into his hotel room, his own words echoing through his mind.

"I trust your instincts, I really do, but honest to God, sometimes I wonder ..."

He barely noticed his surroundings as he took off his poncho and hung it on a rack.

Why? he asked himself.

Why had he spoken to Carly that way? He knew that his words had been unhelpful and his acidic tone had been hurtful. While it was true that her hunch hadn't led them to the killer they were hunting, he knew perfectly well that hunches didn't always pan out. Not his, not hers, not anybody's.

He had long ago accepted that Carly's gut instincts sprang from something more than her training as a profiler. Her so-called hunches were often beyond uncanny. And she was right far more often than she was wrong.

So why was he making so much of her failure this time?

And was it even a failure?

Wasn't there at least a faint possibility they'd actually caught the killer?

Why did he feel so sure they'd gotten the wrong guy?

Lyle stopped his mind from jabbering on and glanced around the room. It looked rather old-fashioned and heavily worn, but marginally functional.

Kind of like myself.

He tossed his go-bag on the wide bed and sat down beside it. Then he just stared into space.

"What the hell's the matter with me?" he muttered aloud.

Of course it was no great mystery. Not so long ago, he'd been reduced to a heap of quivering, helpless rubber by a madman with a needle full of vecuronium.

Carly had very nearly sacrificed her own life to save his.

As if I deserved it, he thought.

The nerve of that kid.

It seemed to Lyle that the awful experience had loosened something in his brain, broken down some of his protective walls. He couldn't keep out the searing images of his previous partner lying at his feet, a gaping, bleeding wound in her chest and a trickle of blood at the edge of her lips.

He couldn't stop her delirious dying words from repeating in his mind.

"Thanks, Lyle. You're always watching out for me. What would I do without ... ?"

Dawn's eyes had faded and her voice fell still.

She seemed to have died thinking Lyle had saved her life, not the other way around. They'd had no chance to rehash that case or talk that gunfight over or say goodbye in any way.

If I could have just talked to her. If I could talk with her now ...

But Lyle had to ask himself how it would go if he could ever talk to Dawn again.

I'd be angry, he realized.

His impatience with Carly just now was nothing in comparison with the rage he felt deep down toward Dawn. She'd been so young, so smart, so funny, and so full of promise, and she'd flung it all away by throwing herself into a bullet's path.

It should have been me, Lyle thought, a painful lump of anguish forming in his throat.

She had no business dying like that.

Lyle stood up from the bed, but he didn't quite know what to do with himself. He walked to the window and looked out. Across the street, a neon sign flickered the name King Tut's Saloon. He'd noticed it there when he'd pulled into the hotel parking lot.

He wondered—had Carly noticed it too? Had it occurred to her that the bar might be a temptation for Lyle? Was that question worrying her right now?

Because it certainly was a temptation.

Most likely his partner was already asleep. It would be easy to put his poncho back on and walk over there and have a drink—a good strong double shot of straight bourbon whiskey.

Just one.

What would be the harm? Carly wouldn't have to find out. Nor would anybody else.

But Lyle knew better than that.

One drink would lead to another and then to another and …

He would never stop. Someone would have to haul him away and dry him out and his FBI career would be over.

Maybe everything would be over.

As if to block those prospects, he kicked his shoes off.

That's not going to happen.

And besides, he reminded himself, he now had a safety net.

He walked over to the bed and unzipped his go-bag. The tinted plastic vial he took out didn't have a label, because it hadn't come with a prescription. All he knew was that the drug was called lorazepam.

A drug no doctor would prescribe for me.

Earlier today he'd assured himself that he wasn't even going to take any of these pills.

Just a safety net.

He'd convinced himself that, somehow, the presence of the container alone would be enough to settle him down.

He knew that was a dumb idea. In fact, that was just the sort of thinking he'd been warned against in substance abuse counseling. But here the vial was, in the palm of his hand, at a moment when it was a struggle not to put his shoes and poncho back on and walk over to King Tut's Saloon and order that whiskey double.

He could probably just get over there before the place closed for the night.

Maybe he'd be lucky and show up just in time for last call. Then he'd get automatically cut off before he could overindulge …

Of course he and Carly had a big, difficult, unpredictable day ahead tomorrow, and he ought to be in bed.

Something clicked in his brain—some sort of decision.

But he wasn't really conscious of what the decision was.

He found himself walking toward the bathroom with the vial in hand. He stood staring at his face in the mirror until he felt like his own expression was accusing him of something. Then he looked away from the mirror and poured a glass of water from the tap.

He popped the bottle open and poured out a single pill. Peering at it closely, he observed how large it looked, and also that it was scored across the middle. His supplier had told him the pill was meant to be cut in half. Half a pill was the intended dosage. So far, that was exactly what he'd done.

But now he wanted more.

Without stopping to think, he put an entire pill in his mouth and swallowed it with a sip of water.

Of course he didn't feel any relief from the action.

It might be a half hour or so before the drug took effect—if it had any affect at all.

Not like a swallow of whiskey.

He remembered how instantly calmed he'd always felt by the friendly, burning sting of whiskey going down his throat. He missed that feeling. And he was sure that just one of these pills wasn't going to have anything like that desired effect.

Without a trace of conscious thought, he poured out another pill and swallowed it as well.

Now maybe I can get some sleep, he thought as he got ready to take a shower.

CHAPTER TWELVE

Valerie Irwin wondered why a penny was lying there on her pillow. She hadn't bothered to turn on the bedroom light, but streetlight spilling through the window reflected off the shiny little coin.

Of course she must have dropped it herself, but she hadn't put her handbag down on the bed.

It didn't matter. It was after midnight. She was still angry, but she hoped that she was finally tired enough to sleep.

She hadn't been home since the funeral for her sister, Lisa, had ended earlier that day. She'd stalked out of the funeral home and headed straight to her car, her own irate words to the other so-called "mourners" still ringing in her ears.

"None of you care about me, any more than you did about Lisa."

Then she'd driven, and driven, and driven.

She'd had no destination, just a desire to keep moving. Away. Even though she knew that she would have to go back to Harmonium.

She'd stuck to the side roads and had even gotten quite lost one or two times. When her gas gauge warned the tank was almost empty, she stopped to fill it up again. She didn't know how far she'd driven, except that she'd pretty much traveled all over the westernmost part of Pennsylvania.

She hadn't thought seriously about going back home until it started raining. She'd been shocked to find herself driving even faster as the roads got slick.

The title of a short story she'd once read popped into her mind: "The Life You Save May Be Your Own." It was a tangled tale of questions about moral behavior, and the title referred to a road sign warning for drivers.

Valerie had known she was not driving carefully.

Even then, it wasn't concern about her own life that made her slow down.

She remembered too well the accident that had left Lisa horribly crippled some 15 years ago—an accident caused by a reckless driver.

The life I save might be some else's, she'd warned herself sternly.

And no one else deserved to suffer like that because of her anger and despair.

So she'd started the long, careful drive home. When she reached the battered, narrow two-story house where she'd grown up and had long since felt herself growing old in, she realized that the life she was used to was over.

As she parked the car and walked to the door, she'd looked away from the wooden wheelchair ramp that sloped down from the small front porch. She'd had it built in the hope that Lisa would recover enough at least to be able to get around in a wheelchair. Instead, she'd worsened and remained hopelessly bedridden for year after year. The ramp had never served any useful purpose, but Lisa had never been able to persuade herself to have it removed.

A part of me was still hoping, I guess, she thought bitterly, standing in her bedroom now.

But hoping for what? some other part of her mind inquired.

Valerie had no answer to that question, any more than she did to the mystery of that single penny on her pillow.

This bedroom hadn't been hers alone, not until very recently. Lisa's hospital bed was still there too. There was even an empty IV stand next to that bed and a side table littered with medicine bottles. Valerie hadn't touched any of those things since Lisa had died.

More stuff I need to get rid of.

But the fact was, the house was full of stuff she really ought to get rid of, and she doubted that she ever could. She walked across the dark room to a closet and opened it. She could barely see inside, but she didn't need to. She could see its contents in her mind. It was full of Lisa's clothes, most of them untouched since before the accident.

How can I throw all this away? she wondered with a deepening stab of grief.

It didn't seem humanly possible. After a day of searing heartache, the shadowy shapes of the clothes were strangely comforting to see.

She started to close the closet door, but stopped.

She heard a strange soft sound. It seemed to be coming from inside the closet—behind her sister's hanging clothes.

It was the sound of breathing.

For a moment Valerie stood frozen, not sure why she didn't run out of the room and the rest of the way out of the house.

My life is in danger.

But she found it weirdly hard to persuade herself to care. She stood there numbly.

Waiting.

But nothing happened.

Finally a new sensation started to creep over her.

It was fear.

Valerie backed a few cautious steps away from the closet.

Run! she commanded herself. *Run now!*

But before she could move, there was a loud rustle from within the closet. A human figure burst out of the dark and pushed her backwards.

In a flash she found herself with her back against the wall with a sharp metal point pricking slightly at her throat. She was staring into a pair of eyes dimly illuminated from the light outside. She was sure she recognized those eyes.

But from where?

Then the man spoke.

"Please, Valerie. Don't be afraid. I don't mean you any harm."

There was a note of genuine kindness in that voice. Why was it so familiar?

Then she remembered where and when she'd heard that voice and seen those eyes.

That man I talked to after the funeral.

He'd approached her when she'd been standing over her sister's coffin after the service was over and the other guests were all moving out of the chapel into the funeral home lobby. He'd asked her for her name, and she'd told him, but she couldn't remember whether he'd mentioned his own name or not. All she knew about him was that he seemed to know just what to say after the horrible ordeal of the service.

"I know it's hard to be alone at a time like now," he'd said. *"It's especially hard to be alone in a roomful of people. People can be so uncaring at times."*

Valerie had breathed a sigh of heartbroken relief at those words.

At last someone understands, she'd thought.

She and the man had only spoken for a few moments, and she couldn't remember much of what they'd said to each other. He'd seemed to be in a hurry to go somewhere else, and he'd been most courteous in his departure. Then Valerie had charged past the other guests, angry and determined not to talk to them.

But that same kindly man was here right now, holding some sort of a blade at her throat.

"What do you want from me?" she asked in a frightened whisper.

"I don't want anything from you," the man said. "I'm only here to help. You told me how much you miss Lisa. I will help you see her again."

This isn't real, Valerie thought.

This has to be a dream.

Now that the idea occurred to her, she was sure of it.

There could be no doubt about it.

None of this was really happening. She was asleep in bed and dreaming about that mysteriously kind stranger who had approached her after Lisa's funeral.

She decided she'd just let the dream run its own course.

"You're going to kill me, aren't you?" she asked calmly.

"Yes. Take this. You're going to need it."

The man squeezed something round and metallic into the palm of her hand—a coin, she thought. Valerie obediently closed her fingers around it.

It must be another penny.

She couldn't think what that might mean.

Even so, she felt a wave of eerie tranquility.

She remembered being told something about what happened when one died in a dream. One died in the real world as well—or at least so it was said. She didn't know whether it was true or not.

Anyway, the prospect didn't trouble her.

There are worse ways to die.

Valerie Irwin barely felt the blade that ended her life.

CHAPTER THIRTEEN

Screams and gunshots and the sounds of breaking glass blasted through the pitch-black darkness, and Carly could smell gunpowder in the air.

But she couldn't see anything at all.

Suddenly the horrible tumult of noise ended and the darkness began to lift, as if some mysterious sunrise was about to appear.

Where am I? *she wondered.* Why am I here?

This was a place she'd never seen before—a smashed window in what looked like a motel, empty shell casings scattered on the pavement, parked cars riddled with bullet holes. A haze of powder smoke hung in the air.

A sprawled body was lying next to one of the vehicles. It was a young woman wearing an FBI jacket. Judging from the gaping wound in her chest, her glassy-eyed expression, and the trickle of blood from her open lips, she was dead.

Then the dead woman's lips started to move.

"Carly …"

Stunned into silence for a moment, Carly realized she'd heard this voice before. A madman had been holding a gun at Lyle's head, demanding that Carly give herself up in his place.

"Don't," *she'd heard this voice say at that near-fatal moment.* "It would kill him with guilt."

"Dawn Metcalf," Carly murmured aloud. "Lyle's partner before me."

The dead woman let out a cough of what sounded like agreement, and more blood dribbled from her mouth. Then her lips moved again, and Carly knelt down to hear her better.

"Lyle's in danger, Carly."

"How do you know?"

"Because I always watch over him. I watch, but I'm powerless to do anything to help him. That's up to you."

"I don't understand."

"He thinks he has to keep you alive. But only you can do that. And sooner or later, maybe you can't either. I wish he could understand. I

stumbled and fell in a bullet's path, that's all. It wasn't his fault. It wasn't my fault either. If only I could tell him. That's just the way life is. And death as well. But now ..."

The dead woman fell silent for a long moment before she spoke again.

"Carly, he's going to hurt himself unless you stop him."

"Hurt himself? How?"

The woman gasped and tried vainly to shape her lips into an answer.

"I can't ... I can't ..."

The voice fell silent again.

"Please tell me—" Carly began.

Before Carly could finish her question, her eyes snapped open.

Her buzzing cell phone had cut her dream vision short. With a sigh, she reached over and picked it up.

This isn't good news, she felt sure.

When she took the call, Lyle's voice was somber.

"Carly, there's been another murder."

"The same killer?"

"Sounds like it. We've got to head over to the crime scene right away. Chief Tallarico is waiting for us there."

"I'll meet you at the car."

They ended the call. With the dead woman's voice was still ringing in her ears, Carly jumped out of bed and began to throw on her clothes.

"I'm powerless to do anything to help him. That's up to you."

Deep in her gut, Carly realized she faced some sort of new and terrible responsibility. But she couldn't think about that right now. A serial killer was on the loose, and he would surely strike again and again. They had to catch him soon.

*

Carly brought up GPS directions and read them as Lyle drove through the streets of Harmonium. She was grateful that it wasn't raining today and the sun was starting to dry the streets.

During the ride, Carly remembered last night's episode in the cemetery ruefully.

"Lyle, I'm sorry," she said.

"For what?"

"For leading us on a wild goose chase last night."

"Well, we didn't have any other leads. We didn't even know for sure that we were dealing with a serial killer. Not then, anyway."

"Even so … I'm sorry."

"Don't be."

Lyle's dull monotone worried Carly, as did the distant look in his eyes. He didn't seem to be still mad at her for her false hunch last night. But she did sense that he was angry about …

Well, something.

Carly remembered what Dawn Metcalf had said in her dream.

"He's going to hurt himself unless you stop him."

What had the dead woman meant by that? The dream vision had been unusually vivid but, just like her sketchier paranormal experiences, it left her with a riddle she had to work out using more mundane methods.

As they turned onto the street where the crime had happened, they faced a discouraging scene.

"Damn it," Lyle growled.

Either word about a serial killer had leaked to the press, or reporters had figured it out on their own. Along with police vehicles and the coroner's van, a couple of TV news vans were parked in front of the house they were headed for. Cops were trying to keep several reporters from breaking through the police tape to get inside for a look at the crime scene.

Lyle parked as close to the house as he could. When he and Carly got out of the car, reporters clustered around them.

"Are you FBI agents?" a camera-wielding man inquired,

Neither Carly nor Lyle took out their badges to identify themselves.

"We don't have anything to say at this time," Lyle replied.

Other reporters yelled out their questions.

"But isn't there a serial killer at large?"

"Isn't that why you've been called in from Quantico?"

"And does the fact that you're already here mean you knew there was a serial killer yesterday? Before the current victim was killed?"

"Why wasn't the public warned?"

Lyle simply repeated what he'd said before.

"We don't have anything to say at this time."

Lyle and Carly pushed past the reporters toward the house. The clamoring reporters reminded her of the urgency of this case, and of something Mayor Freelander had said.

"I decided I'd make Harmonium the kind of town my grandfather could be proud of if he came back. And I've been trying to do that all my life."

She was sure the mayor wasn't the only person in Harmonium who felt that way. Now that they knew for certain there was a serial killer on the loose, Carly knew that the mayor's hopes were in serious jeopardy, and the hopes of many other people as well. A lot was truly at stake in this case.

The house was an older building with a small yard that was more mud than grass. A wooden wheelchair ramp extended from the front porch, and Chief Tallarico was standing on that porch with his arms crossed and a scowl on his face.

"I guess it's the real thing after all, then," he said flatly.

Of course Carly knew he was embarrassed about his own skepticism yesterday.

"I've still got my doubts about it," he'd told them.

There wasn't much room for doubt now.

"I guess I'm going to have to make some kind of statement to the press," Tallarico said.

"Yeah, but not just this minute," Lyle replied. "Show us where it happened."

Tallarico led them into the house's small living room, where a uniformed officer with a pencil and notepad was quietly interviewing a stunned-looking middle-aged man who was sitting on the sofa.

"Who's that guy?" Lyle quietly asked the Tallarico.

"The victim's brother," Tallarico said. "He found the body a short time ago."

Lyle stopped walking for a moment and stared at the man. Then they continued on into the bedroom.

It was a small room—uncomfortably small for the double bed and the hospital bed that took up much of the space. A side table was crowded with medicine bottles. A closet door stood open. The dead woman was lying on the floor next to a wall. Her throat had obviously been cut, and blood and had splashed all around her. With one of his assistants at his side, Coroner Simon Russo was kneeling over the sprawled-out corpse peering closely at the neck wound.

The victim appeared to have been about the same age as the man they'd passed in the living room. Her eyes were wide open, and Carly was struck by what seemed to be an utter lack of surprise on her face. But as she had with the photos of Sarah Tooley's corpse, she reminded herself not to read too much into a dead person's expression.

"Agents Ramsey and See are here," Tallarico said to the coroner.

Dr. Russo glanced up at them, barely pausing from his examination. His normally ruddy face appeared even redder from evident frustration.

"I'm glad you're here," Russo said. "But I don't suppose we need your expertise to tell us what's going on. We've got a serial killer for sure. Damn, but I wish I'd spent more time examining that homeless man's wound."

Tallarico shuffled his feet and said, "Yeah, and I wish I hadn't tried to convince myself it was something else."

Lyle let out a grunt that seemed to suggest he wasn't going to jump in with a lot of sympathy.

"Tell us what happened," he said to Tallarico.

"The victim's name was Valerie Irwin. She was a single woman who spent many years caring for her invalid sister, as you can see by the wheelchair ramp and the hospital bed and all these medications. Her sister died a few days ago."

"Can you estimate the time of death for the victim?"

"Not for certain. But judging by the corpse's temperature, my guess would be an hour or two after midnight. And it was done with a very sharp, pointed blade. The same as the other killings—a box cutter or some other kind of utility knife, probably."

Lyle asked Tallarico, "Any idea how he got into the house?"

"My guess it was somebody she knew."

"What makes you think that?"

"Well, I don't see any sign of a struggle. Maybe it was a boyfriend she thought would be spending the night with her."

Carly was skeptical about that. There had been signs of a struggle at the scene of the homeless man's murder, and she and Lyle were quite sure that Sarah Tooley had been killed by an intruder. This was the same M.O., and a boyfriend would be inconsistent. So would any involvement of the brother.

"I don't know about that," Lyle said, looking around the room.

I don't know either, Carly thought.

But as she looked around, her eye was caught by the open closet door. She exchanged a glance and a nod with Lyle, who walked toward the closet.

"Was the closet open when the woman's brother found her body?" Lyle asked.

Tallarico nodded.

Lyle probed among the hanging clothes with his hand, then stooped down and rubbed his hand on the floor. Lyle glanced at Carly again, and they nodded again in agreement. She knew exactly what he'd found.

"The killer was an intruder," Carly said. "Whether she knew him or not, she didn't expect to find him here."

"What makes you think that?" Tallarico asked.

"The clothes aren't hanging quite straight," Lyle said. "And the closet floor is streaked with a little dried mud. The killer entered the house while the victim was out. He probably picked a lock to get in, since that's what he seems to have done at Sarah Tooley's apartment. He hid here behind all the clothes. It rained last night, and the soles of his feet were muddy."

Tallarico squinted with interest.

"So he took her by surprise from the closet?"

"That's right," Lyle said with a nod. "And she'd just arrived at home herself."

"How do you know that? Couldn't the killer have stayed hidden for hours while she was in the house?"

Again, Carly understood what Lyle was getting at. She'd already come to the same conclusion.

"Look at how the victim is dressed," she said. "These aren't the kinds of clothes you wear to lounge around the house. She'd been at some kind of formal gathering or other."

"At one or two o'clock in the morning?"

"Maybe she got together with friends after whatever occasion she was dressed up for," she said. "She could've gone out for a drink or something."

Lyle walked back to the corpse and pointed to her closed hand.

"It looks like she's holding something. What do you guess it might be?"

Carly shivered at the obvious answer.

The coroner pried apart the victim's stiff fingers, and sure enough, there was a penny in her hand.

"This is definitely our killer's calling card," Tallarico said with a shudder.

"But what is it supposed to mean?" Russo asked.

Lyle crouched down next to the body and peered at the penny.

"It may not be a message for us. It might have been something more private—some kind of communication with each victim …"

As Lyle continued, Carly knew that what he was saying was pure speculation now. Talking through the possibilities helped them focus on unanswered questions.

Her attention began to drift. As always at a murder scene, she wondered whether she could make any kind of contact with the victim's spirit. With the three men crowded around the corpse, touching the body itself was clearly not an option.

She walked over to the closet and stood staring at the somewhat rumpled clothing inside. They struck her as an outdated collection.

This is where the killer took her by surprise.

When Carly reached out to touch a blouse, she felt a charge of mysterious energy.

Keep control.

It wouldn't do to cry out or fall in a heap on the floor. She stiffened herself to absorb the full force of the impending vision.

She closed her eyes, and a familiar image filled her mind.

CHAPTER FOURTEEN

Carly was again standing over a closed wooden coffin.

She could see nothing else, and nothing at all was happening.

The vision was eerily similar to the one she'd had yesterday in Sarah Tooley's bedroom. So as she'd done before, Carly knocked on the coffin lid.

"Go away," a woman's voice said from inside the coffin.

But that wasn't Sarah Tooley's voice. It was a distinctly different woman.

Carly remembered that, outside of her vision, she was actually in a new victim's room.

"Is this Valerie Irwin?" Carly asked silently.

"Go away, I said. You'll wake up Lisa. She's finally getting some sleep. And I need peace and quiet myself."

"But I want to help."

"You don't belong here, whoever you are."

"But—"

"I mean it. Go away."

Carly stood wavering. Why did the spirits of the dead women in this case want nothing to do with her? They had been murdered, after all.

Don't these victims even want me to know who killed them?

Then the vision changed, much as it had before.

She became aware of a salty dampness in the breeze and the cries of seagulls in the air. Again, she stepped back from the coffin and saw that it was just one of many coffins stacked up in the shape of a pyramid. And that stack of coffins was the cargo of a modern-day ferryboat.

And again, looking out over the railing, she saw a vast sea with gravestones and monuments rising out of it.

What is this place? she wondered. *Why do I keep returning here?*

As the vision and the noises began to fade. Carly opened her eyes and found herself staring at the clothes in Valerie Irwin's closet. This was where the killer had hidden, but she hadn't gained any information from this victim—not about him, not about any of his murders.

The voices of three men in the room became audible again and she turned to face them.

"Can my team take the body to the van now?" Dr. Russo was asking.

"Not while there are reporters outside," Tallarico said. "Give me a chance to make a statement to them. Then my guys can clear them out of your way."

"Let's get the body ready to go," Dr. Russo said to his assistant.

"Right," the young man replied.

Lyle rose to his feet and asked Tallarico, "What's the brother's name?"

"Dwayne Irwin."

"I want to talk to him now."

Carly followed Lyle and Tallarico into the living room. The cop who had been interviewing Dwayne Irwin seemed to be finishing up his work. He folded up his notebook and followed Tallarico outside, where the chief was going to make his statement to the reporters.

Carly and Lyle pulled up chairs in front of the sofa, sat facing Dwayne Irwin, and produced their badges.

"I'm Special Agent Carly See with the FBI," she said, "and this is my partner, Special Agent Lyle Ramsey. We're sorry for your loss, Mr. Irwin."

"Thanks," Irwin replied in a voice still hoarse from shock. "Can I go now?"

"We've just got a few questions of our own," Carly told him.

"I've already answered a lot of questions."

"Just bear with us, please. We'll try to keep this short."

Carly and Lyle both took out their notepads.

"Could you tell us how you found your sister's body?" Lyle asked.

The man's mouth opened, but for a few moments he seemed to have trouble forcing out any words.

"It's like I told the officer," he finally said. "I called her early this morning to check up on her. Our sister Lisa died a few days ago. Her funeral was just yesterday, and I was worried about how Valerie was doing. She didn't answer her phone, so I came by her house. I found the front door not quite closed, so I got worried. So I came on inside and …"

Irwin's voice faded and his face twitched with pain at the awful memory.

"What time was yesterday's funeral?" Lyle asked.

"Ten-thirty in the morning."

Carly noticed that Lyle squinted skeptically. She, too, found something odd about what the man was saying.

"Where was the funeral held?" she asked.

"At the Garrison Funeral Home."

"Who presided over the service?" Lyle asked.

"Pastor Miles Lindsay. He's the pastor at Immanuel Lutheran Church."

Lyle tapped his notepad with his pencil for a moment.

"Was your sister a regular churchgoer?" he asked.

Irwin's body shifted awkwardly.

"Uh, no. Lisa couldn't go much of anywhere. She was an invalid, you know, and she couldn't get around. She was badly injured in a terrible car accident 15 years ago. She finally died from those injuries. After the accident, Valerie didn't go back to church either."

"So whose idea was it to bring in Pastor Lindsay?" Lyle asked.

"Mine, I guess," Irwin said with a shrug. "Immanuel Lutheran was where our family—Mom and Dad and Valerie and Lisa and I—had always gone before. I thought … well, I just decided we just ought to have some kind of service with a preacher presiding."

"How did Valerie feel about this decision?"

"Uh, she was fine with it, I guess."

Carly exchanged a suspicious glance with Lyle.

"You guess?" she asked.

"Well, I mean, she didn't … raise any objection."

As she jotted down notes, Carly sensed that the man wasn't telling the truth, and she was sure her partner did too. Lyle's scowl had deepened, and his eyes were now locked on Irwin's.

"How many people attended the funeral?" he asked.

"Oh, just a few of us. Eight people, I think."

"Could you tell us who they were?" Carly asked.

"Well, there were me and my wife and son. And an uncle of ours, and his wife. And some school friends."

"School friends?" Lyle asked.

"You know, from Lisa's childhood or high school or college. I'm sure the funeral home can give you a list of who signed the register."

"How were your sister's spirits during the service?" Lyle asked. "Her mood, I mean?"

Irwin's face had reddened considerably.

"She was sad, of course … but …"

He fell silent for a moment, then added, "But we all did our best to console her."

Lyle leaned forward in his chair.

"What can you tell us about Valerie's activities yesterday after the funeral?" he asked.

"I—I don't know anything about that."

"You weren't in touch with her at all?"

"No."

"You didn't try to get in touch?"

"Uh, no."

Carly now heard a sullen growl in Lyle's voice. She, too, was sure this was a lie.

"Mr. Irwin, I'm sure you know it's against the law to lie to a law enforcement official," Lyle said.

Dwayne Irwin began sputtering now.

"Why—why would I lie about any of this? My God, do you consider me a suspect? Is that what this is all about?"

Lyle jabbed his finger at Irwin.

"The police are sure to check all of Valerie's phone messages for yesterday," he said. "What do you think they'll find?"

Irwin's mouth hung open, and he made no reply.

"Never mind, I think I can tell you," Lyle said. "You called her repeatedly all day long, trying desperately to reach her. Finally this morning you got worried enough to come here and check on her."

Dwayne Irwin slumped forward as if he'd been punched in the stomach.

"I don't understand what this has to do with anything," he said, a sob rising up in his throat.

"That's up to my partner and me to determine," Lyle said. "All I want is for you to tell us the truth."

Irwin took out a handkerchief and wiped his eyes.

"The funeral was … awful," he said. "Valerie was so angry. She stood in front of us and accused us of …"

He shook his head miserably.

"Well, everything she said was true. We'd left her to carry the whole responsibility of caring for Lisa after the accident. We just took her for granted, didn't want to be bothered, and some of us never even spoke to her or Lisa for years. And when she finished talking yesterday, no one approached her to comfort her or apologize or … We just tried to pretend … We were too ashamed to even …"

Dwayne Irwin's voice faded for a moment.

"I spent the rest of the day feeling guilty," he went on. "I called her over and over again, and I left messages begging her to call me back, but she never did, and this morning I finally came here and …"

His voice faded again.

"But I don't know what this has to do with anything," he finally murmured.

That's a good question, Carly thought.

The motives for Dwayne Irwin's deception now seemed obvious, and she doubted that they had anything to do with murder. Meanwhile, she found herself startled by Lyle's ruthless prodding.

What was the point?

Carly knew there was one last question that needed to be asked.

"Mr. Irwin, did either you or your sister know Sarah Tooley?"

"Was she one of the other victims?" Dwayne Irwin asked.

Carly nodded.

"Not that I know of, no," the man said. "I mean, the name doesn't ring a bell."

Lyle got up from his chair and growled almost inaudibly.

"Thank you for your time, Mr. Irwin. Again, we're sorry for your loss."

As they stepped away from the devastated man, Carly couldn't keep her feelings to herself.

"Lyle, what the hell was that all about?" she whispered.

"I just hate it when they lie."

"Yeah, but—"

"Carly, let's not do this right now," Lyle interrupted. "Let's go somewhere to get some coffee and figure out how we're going to proceed."

But as they approached the front door, they heard a familiar voice from outside—and it wasn't Chief Tallarico's voice.

"I just want you to know I share your outrage, and I promise you justice will be done, and …"

"Oh, crap," Lyle said.

CHAPTER FIFTEEN

Sure enough, when she and Lyle stepped into the open doorway, Carly saw that Mayor Ike Freelander had arrived and was making his own statement to the reporters. For this occasion, the rotund mayor had donned a suit jacket and a multicolored tie. Standing silently at his side, Chief Tallarico looked cowed and irritated as the mayor held forth to the reporters.

Carly realized that Freelander must have made a beeline here as soon as he got the news. And Tallarico hadn't been expecting him.

The mayor continued, "I promise you I won't rest until this madman is off our streets and Harmonium is safe again. And Chief Tallarico is here to offer the same promise on behalf of the police."

Freelander glanced back and saw Lyle and Carly standing on the porch.

He said to the reporters, "Fortunately we've got the very best investigators on the job—BAU Special Agents Ramsey and See. They arrived here yesterday at the first hint that a serial killer was at large."

The reporters began to speak up.

"You say they arrived here at the 'first hint' of a serial killer. Why wasn't the public warned of this possibility?"

"Why isn't the killer in custody already?"

"Why was another murder allowed to happen?"

"Frankly, we didn't have enough information to alert the public," the mayor told them. "I'm sure you understand that we didn't want to cause a panic. This latest murder is most unfortunate. But Agents Ramsey and See have assured me that it could not possibly have been prevented."

Carly and Lyle exchanged startled glances.

"We *'assured'* him?" Carly whispered.

That was obviously impossible. This was the first time they'd even seen the mayor so far today.

"This old political hack has got some nerve," Lyle muttered back.

But it seemed that the mayor was just getting warmed up.

"Agents Ramsey and See have personally promised me to close this case soon—almost certainly before the day is over. And *absolutely* before this monster claims another victim. Before tomorrow, Harmonium will be rid of this threat. And we can all get back to the task of restoring our fair city to its former glory."

He waved toward Carly and Lyle and said, "Perhaps the two of you would be so kind as to say a few words about the status of the case."

Carly winced at the trap the mayor had caught them in, probably quite deliberately. There was simply nothing meaningful either she or Lyle could say at this point. She was sure the mayor had fully intended to put them on the spot because he didn't fully trust their commitment. Yesterday he'd said, *"I want to make sure you're serious about your job."* Now he wanted to hear them make a public statement affirming their determination to stop the killer.

But in situations like this, Carly could usually count on Lyle to improvise, offer the media some kind of reassurance, and maybe even to subtly put the mayor in his place.

Instead, her partner just commented tersely, "We've got work to do."

Then he turned and walked away.

The mayor's mouth dropped open, and Tallarico's eyes widened with surprise.

For a moment even the reporters gawked silently. By the time they started waving their arms and shouting questions, Lyle was halfway back to their vehicle.

Carly trotted along and caught up with him. This was unusual behavior, but she didn't see any point in trying to talk him into going back and answering questions for the local press. In his current state of mind Lyle would likely end up completely undercutting the city officials, and not at all subtly.

"Where are we going?" she asked as they reached the car.

"To get something to eat, just like I said," Lyle replied through clenched teeth.

What's the matter with him today? she wondered.

As Lyle silently drove them through the streets of Harmonium, her anxiety was rising. She remembered noticing something worrisome last night as they'd pulled into the hotel parking lot.

There had been a bar on the opposite side of the street from the hotel—the flickering neon sign had read King Tut's Saloon. It was in clear view from the window of her own room, so it had been visible from Lyle's as well.

She had to wonder again if her partner had rushed back to work too soon after his traumatic paralysis at the hands of a murderous madman.

Did he slip out last night for a drink?

Or for a lot of drinks?

She pushed the thoughts aside, but they wouldn't disappear. It was the worst possible scenario, but …

I promised Chief Voss I'd alert him if Lyle started drinking again.

Had the time come for her to do that?

How could she know for sure, one way or the other?

I could just ask, I guess.

But somehow she couldn't force herself to do that.

Lyle pulled the car into the lot of an innocuous-looking fast food restaurant. They went inside together, ordered coffee and pancakes, and sat down at one of the plastic tables.

"So what do you suggest we do next?" Lyle asked.

Carly felt a few ideas taking shape, but other questions still cluttered her mind. She had to deal with those first.

"Lyle, what were you trying to accomplish back there at the house?"

"What do you mean?"

"I mean with the victim's brother. Why did you grill him like that?"

"For information, obviously."

"Yeah, but … you got so personal with him about his issues with Valerie. Why did you need to know everything about how he'd felt at the funeral, and how he spent the rest of the day?"

"Because I knew he was lying about something."

"But what's the point about all that stuff that came out?"

"Carly, just think about it, OK? We learned that Valerie Irwin was bitter and isolated, at odds with everybody in her family and all her former friends. Some of them hadn't spoken to her for years. There were a lot of hard feelings in that family. And hard feelings can get deadly."

Lyle drummed his fingers on the table impatiently.

"I don't know about you, but I feel like I know the victim a lot better now. She'd given up on religion years ago, mostly because of how she saw her sister suffer for years and years on end. Even so, her brother insisted on a proper funeral with a preacher presiding. Other friends and family members probably pushed for that too. And it made Valerie mad. And I'll bet she told them so."

Carly found herself nodding in agreement. The spirit who had spoken to her was certainly angry.

"And who could blame her?" Lyle went on. "After years of neglect, suddenly the whole gang wanted to get in on the act. Nobody listened to Valerie, who probably wanted Lisa's remains cremated and scattered without any ceremony at all. Nobody cared about her feelings—or Lisa's either, for that matter. They never had cared."

Lyle paused for a moment.

"Dwayne Irwin was telling the truth about one thing," he continued. "He really had no idea what Valerie did during the whole day after the funeral. All he knew was, he couldn't reach her by phone."

He chuckled grimly.

"But I can tell you what she did that whole time. I know it because it's exactly what I would do. She got in her car and just started driving. She didn't go anywhere in particular, just drove and drove and drove until she got too tired to drive. And by the time she got home …"

His voice faded, then he shook his head.

"She didn't want to live, Carly. She was just so damn sick of everything, she probably wasn't even scared when she opened that closet and found a man there waiting to kill her. She might even have felt relieved."

He's sounding like the Lyle I know, Carly thought.

Lyle was playing to his strengths again—and they were the sort of strengths Carly wished she had herself. She envied his intuitive ability to infer theories and possibilities, not from supernatural visitations but from hard facts. She knew that a lot of that skill was based on his remarkable powers of empathy.

Carly didn't doubt his hunch that Valerie Irwin had gone out driving for hours and hours after the funeral. And Lyle had come to this conclusion because he'd been able to put himself in the victim's shoes, to really understand something about the pain and frustration she'd felt not only over her sister's death, but over years of coldness and indifference from friends and family.

But of course, Valerie Irwin hadn't been the only victim.

"Everything you're saying makes sense," Carly said. "But what does any of it have to do with the other two murders?"

"That's the part I haven't worked out yet. Have you got any ideas?"

Carly's brow knitted with thought. She flashed back to the impressions she'd gotten from two of the victims, and certain things they'd said from inside their coffins.

"Soon I'll be with Amber," Sarah had said. *"She's waiting for me."*

"You'll wake up Lisa," Valerie had said when Carly knocked on

the coffin lid. *"She's finally getting some sleep."*

Carly realized the two murdered women did have something in common.

They were both grieving for dead loved ones.

Of course Carly couldn't explain to Lyle that she'd actually talked with two spirits of the dead, but she needed to broach the subject somehow.

"Lyle, do you remember something Sarah Tooley's husband told us? He said Sarah had been taking the death of her friend really hard. He said she'd felt guilty about not being able to spend more time with her in the hospital."

Lyle's eyes lit up a little.

"That's right. What did he say the friend's name was?"

"Amber. Amber Jordan."

Lyle leaned across the table toward her.

"So two of the victims were in mourning. Maybe that means something."

"We still don't know about the homeless man. But maybe we can find a link between those two women."

She took out her cellphone and ran a search: "Amber Jordan obituary."

"Here's something," she said excitedly. "Amber Jordan's funeral was held three and a half weeks ago at the Immanuel Lutheran Church. The presiding pastor was Miles Lindsay."

Lyle's eyes widened.

"The same preacher who conducted Lisa Irwin's service," he said.

"That's right. And we know Valerie Irwin attended her sister's funeral, and it's a good bet Sarah Tooley attended her friend's funeral. Even if there's nothing else connecting them, there's the preacher. Of course it could be a coincidence."

Lyle was eating faster now.

"But maybe not," he said. "We'd better pay the good pastor a visit. Good thinking, Carly."

"Thanks."

As they finished up their meals in silence, Carly was relieved by Lyle's renewed attitude. Even so, she couldn't take her eyes off his tired face. Lyle's eyelids looked heavy, and the flesh beneath his eyes was swollen and red.

Lyle finally seemed to notice Carly's gaze. He took a long, deep breath before he spoke.

"Carly, I haven't been drinking,"

She almost dropped her coffee cup.

"I know you've been worried about that," he stated flatly. "And I know Chief Voss has too. He talked to you about it, didn't he?'

Carly nodded mutely.

"Well, I guess part of me isn't happy about all that," Lyle admitted. "But I can't blame either one of you. You're both my friends. So I'm kind of grateful, I guess. But from now on, when you've got something like that on your mind, just ask it outright, OK?"

"OK."

Carly felt a strange mixture of embarrassment and relief at the way Lyle had called her out. Even so, she found herself flashing back to the ominous words of his long-dead partner.

"Carly, he's going to hurt himself unless you stop him."

As she finished up her coffee, Carly was wondering what she would be able to do if the spirit of Dawn Metcalf was right about that.

CHAPTER SIXTEEN

The buzzing of Carly's cell phone interrupted her speculations about Lyle and the spirit of his deceased partner. She was a bit surprised at her pleasant tingle when she saw who was contacting her.

It was a text from Mark Lawson.

His message was simple and to the point.

Just hoping you're well. No need to get back to me. Looking forward to seeing you when you get back. Hope you're having luck with the case.

As usual, Carly had been so immersed in the case that she'd given little thought to anyone or anything beyond it. Although she'd had lunch with Mark just yesterday, the message felt like a voice reaching out from her distant past.

Even so, it made her feel good to see his words.

"What are you smiling about?" Lyle asked, glancing at her from behind the steering wheel.

Carly was even more startled to realize how transparent her reaction must have been. She felt herself redden a little as she replied.

"Nothing."

"Huh, That's not a 'nothing' grin."

When she didn't respond, Lyle cut his eyes toward her again and then let out a laugh.

"Don't try to delude an old profiler. I can read you like a book."

"It was just a note from a … a childhood friend. Nothing really personal."

"So why are you all pink-cheeked now? There's something romantic going on, isn't there?"

Carly felt like an embarrassed teenager. She was pleased, though, that Lyle was momentarily emerging from his personal shadows—enough to notice her reaction and tease her about it, at least.

"Thanks for asking. But it's too soon to tell."

"Not too soon for it to be a real question though."

"I just don't know …"

"Well, make up your mind, why don't you?"

"It's not that simple."

"Huh. I've heard that before."

This time, Carly didn't reply at all, and her partner didn't push his questions again. But she could see that Lyle was grinning as he drove them through Harmonium on the way to their next destination.

The truth was that the prospect of including Mark in her life really *wasn't* that simple. It felt very complicated, in fact. She remembered the startling turn their conversation had taken when he'd told her he was thinking about taking a job in the D.C. area.

"Would it be ... OK with you if we saw a lot more of each other?" he'd asked.

It had been a bigger question than it sounded. Carly knew Mark's choices about his own professional future might hinge on her reply, and she didn't feel ready to accept that responsibility.

It hardly seems fair after all these years, she thought.

This was no longer a teenage flirtation. They were both adults, and they were both haunted by a past that left so much unresolved.

Clearly Mark was well aware of that issue. At lunch he'd observed that Megan's disappearance still affected them.

"There are three people here at this table, aren't there?"

Of course Mark had no idea that Carly was dealing with the questions of whether Megan was still alive, and where she might be if she were alive. He didn't know that Carly had been out a few days ago looking for traces of her missing sister.

Which brought Carly's internal struggle around to the most important issue.

He doesn't know about ... me.

Just keeping her gift hidden from Lyle was proving to be impossible, and she knew she was soon going to have to stop trying.

How much has he guessed already?

She didn't know. But if she couldn't keep this secret from Lyle, how could she possibly hide it from a romantic partner?

That very dilemma had always kept Carly's attachments somewhat restrained and uncomplicated by expectations of any shared future. Although a couple of her relationships had been intense, those had been short-lived. Either the guy developed freaky suspicions about her and bailed on her in a panic, or she got nervous that he was getting too close to the truth about her and ended things herself.

And anyway, she knew that Mark wasn't looking for a fling. He was a sweet guy, and Carly couldn't help thinking he deserved better than that.

Maybe I should just keep my distance from him, she thought.

But in her heart, she knew she didn't want to do that. Like Mark, she was looking forward to the two of them getting together …

When?

After this case was solved, of course. But when would that be?

Maybe, Carly hoped, they were going to get a break right now. Then she could get back to Mark with a positive answer.

Lyle pulled their vehicle into a parking lot next to a traditional-looking red brick church. Next to the church, a tidy, pleasant bungalow with a stone porch and foundation was obviously the rectory. It was a picture-perfect little building, with neat gardens and well-trimmed shrubbery on both sides of a small porch.

"Let's check there first," Lyle said, indicating the rectory.

When they got out of the car and walked up onto the porch, they saw that the glass-paned front door displayed a welcome sign. Lyle opened the door, and they stepped into a comfortable foyer with an array of beige chairs, scenic paintings on the wall, and a wooden reception desk.

Sitting at the desk was a middle-aged woman dressed in pastel colors and wearing reading glasses attached to a beaded chain. The nameplate on her desk read Mallory Butler.

"Can I help you?" the receptionist asked, looking up from some paperwork.

Carly and Lyle produced their badges and introduced themselves.

Lyle added, "We're here to talk to Reverend Miles Lindsay, if he's available."

The woman's smile shifted from cordial to frozen-in-place. Her eyes widened.

After a moment's hesitation, she asked nervously, "May I ask … what is your business with the reverend?"

"We'd prefer to discuss that with him privately," Lyle said.

The woman stammered, "I—I'm afraid that won't be possible."

Something's wrong here, Carly thought.

She and Lyle exchanged a split-second glance. It was obvious to both of them that for some reason, this woman was trying to cover for the pastor.

"Why won't it be possible?" Lyle asked the woman.

"He's—he's not in right now."

“Then perhaps we can catch him over at the church?”

“I don’t know about that. I doubt it.”

“When do you expect him back?”

“I have no idea.”

Carly saw a familiar mischievous twitch around the edges of Lyle’s lips as he put his hands in his pockets.

“Fortunately, we’re not in any hurry,” he said. “We’ll just wait here until he comes back.”

The woman glanced nervously toward an archway that led into the house.

He’s right here in the house, all right, Carly thought.

“I’m afraid that’s not such a good idea,” the woman replied to Lyle.

“Why not?”

“Well—it might be a long wait. I don’t want to … cause you any inconvenience.”

“Oh, it’s no inconvenience at all,” Lyle said, sitting down in a comfortable armchair. “We work for the federal government. We’re as patient as can be. Thanks for your concern, though.”

Carly sat down in a chair next to Lyle’s. They both took out their cellphones and acted as though they were using them for some sort of work.

With a brief huffing sound, the receptionist tried to pretend to keep working herself. The only sound in the room for a minute or so was her shuffling of papers, but she was looking more and more nervous.

Finally the woman got up from her desk. Without a glance in the agents’ direction, she slipped out through the archway into the main house.

A few more minutes passed.

Then a tall, slender man in his late 30s walked into the room. He was wearing a white clergyman’s collar. He was closely followed by the receptionist, who sat down at her desk and gazed at Carly and Lyle warily.

Then the man turned toward Carly and Lyle.

He’s a cool one, she realized.

His demeanor was unreadable.

CHAPTER SEVENTEEN

Carly didn't see any trace of anxiety on the pastor's face. He cut a daunting figure, with a jutting chin and hawk-like eyebrows that she'd somehow come to associate with preachers and military men—a look of almost caricatured uprightness. As he extended his hand for both Carly and Lyle to shake, his expression was calm, cordial, and distant.

"Hello, I'm Miles Lindsay, the pastor here at Immanuel Lutheran Church. Mallory here says you're from the FBI."

Carly and Lyle produced their badges and introduced themselves again.

"This must be about some very serious matter," the pastor said.

Even though Carly found faces like his hard to read, she thought she detected a flicker of uneasiness in the man's expression.

"Yes, it is, reverend," Lyle replied. "And we'd like to talk to you about it privately, if you don't mind."

"Of course, of course. Come on into my office."

Carly and Lyle followed him into a small office that was decorated in subdued shades of tan and gray. A wall of bookshelves displayed appropriate religious books. Another wall was covered with photographs of the pastor with various people, along with his educational credentials and certificates of community appreciation. An amateurish painting of a religious scene was framed in gold. Sunlight shining in through a window did nothing to relieve the somber atmosphere of the pastor's domain.

Pastor Lindsay offered a couple of chairs to Lyle and Carly, then sat down behind his wide desk.

"I'm glad you've got time to talk to us," Lyle remarked with a note of irony in his voice. "Your receptionist gave us the impression that you weren't in."

The pastor let out a rather artificial-sounding chuckle.

"Yes, I'm afraid you caught Mallory in one of her overly-protective moods. She takes her duties as 'guardian at the gates' a bit too earnestly, I fear."

Carly sensed that there was more to the woman's evasiveness than that. She hadn't appeared nervous until they'd identified themselves as

FBI.

"What may I do for you?" the pastor inquired.

"Are you aware that there's a serial killer at large here in Harmonium?" Lyle asked.

The pastor's forehead wrinkled.

"Why, no," he said. "How terribly shocking."

His voice didn't sound especially shocked to Carly. But then, she sensed that this man wasn't easily alarmed.

But is he lying? Carly wondered.

"We've only been sure of it since this morning," Lyle said. "There have been three victims so far, over a period of about a week."

"I haven't had a chance to check the news today, but I would have heard if one of my parishioners was involved." He appeared lost in thought again, then asked rather abruptly, "What does it have to do with me?"

"My partner and I are wondering whether you might have any personal connection to last night's victim," Lyle said. "Her name was Valerie Irwin."

Pastor Lindsay scratched his chin.

"I don't recognize that name," he said.

"Are you sure?" Carly put in. "What about her sister, Lisa Irwin?"

"Why, yes," the pastor admitted. "I do know her name, at least. She wasn't a parishioner either, but her family wanted me to perform her service over at the Garrison Funeral Home. Such a hard life she had, after such a terrible accident. I presided over her funeral just yesterday. So many years living as an invalid, poor thing. Death was truly a blessing—she's in the Lord's hands now. And now that I remember it, her sister *was* there. And yes, her name was Valerie. And you're saying this sister was a murder victim? My goodness, how terrible!"

"What about the previous victim?" Lyle asked, "Her name was Sarah Tooley."

"No, I don't believe I have a parishioner with that name either."

"She had a close friend named Amber Jordan," Carly added.

"Oh, dear," the pastor said with seemingly mild surprise. "Yes, Amber was a parishioner here. Poor soul, she also suffered a great deal before she went to her maker. Leukemia, I believe it was. We held our services for her right here at the church a few days ago."

"Are you sure you don't remember Sarah Tooley?" Lyle said. "We want to know whether she attended Amber Jordan's funeral."

Pastor Lindsay rolled his eyes slightly.

"I'm afraid you're asking for a bit of a miracle," he said. "I conduct so many services of one kind or another. I don't always know everyone who attends, and I might not remember a name even if there was a brief introduction."

"Don't families usually have a guest list?" Carly asked. "Or at least have visitors sign a guest book?"

"Of course, if they want to. It's optional."

"Could you check for us, please?"

"Check to see if she came to the funeral, you mean? Oh, I don't think so, no. There's a question of sanctity, isn't there? And legal privilege."

Lyle leaned forward in his chair. Carly sensed from his expression that he was suspicious of the pastor—and also more than a little impatient.

Stay cool, Lyle, she wanted to say.

"Reverend, I doubt very much that any kind of privilege applies here, and I'm pretty sure you don't think so either," Lyle said. "Clergy privilege is specifically about one-on-one communications between you and your parishioners. A funeral is a public matter, not exactly a private communication. Now we could double-check on the legality of this issue if you prefer, but I can't help thinking it would be easier for you to just help us out."

Pastor Lindsay's lips twisted oddly. Then he reached over and touched his intercom button.

"Mallory, could you please check the guest list for Amber Jordan's funeral? We'd like to know if it includes a woman named Sarah Tooley."

"I'll do that, Miles," Mallory replied. "It will just take a minute."

Carly mentally noted that the receptionist called Lindsay by his first name, not by his title.

Probably nothing unusual there, she told herself.

Even so, she was still curious about the receptionist's visible uneasiness. Was Mallory's concern entirely for the pastor's benefit, or for her own, or were the two of them hiding something?

"While we wait, let's get back to Valerie Irwin," Lyle said. "Could you tell us anything about her behavior during the funeral service?"

Lindsay drummed his fingers on the desk for a moment.

"To be truthful, she was angry when she spoke," he finally said. "She had harsh words for the others who were present. She accused them of neglecting both her and Lisa during the years she'd spent caring for sister. She felt they were hypocrites for even being there."

Carly shivered as she remembered Valerie's voice during that vision, telling her to stop knocking on the coffin lid.

"You'll wake up Lisa. She's finally getting some sleep. And I need some peace and quiet myself."

Lindsay leaned back and swiveled in his chair.

"But she was more than just angry. She was in despair. She said she envied her sister. She said she had no reason now to go on living. Poor woman, I was afraid she might try something desperate, and after the service I tried to comfort her, but she wanted none of that. I was very worried about her."

He stopped suddenly, and then demanded, "What makes you so sure that Valerie Irwin was a murder victim? If her despair was as deep as it appeared ..."

"We're sure," Carly replied sharply, remembering the identical neat slashes to the victim's throats.

Then came Mallory's voice over the intercom.

"Yes, there was a Sarah Tooley at the funeral."

"Thank you," the reverend replied.

Questions began to swarm in Carly's mind.

"Does knowing this jog your memory, reverend?" she asked. "Do you remember Sarah Tooley now?"

"I'm afraid not," Lindsay said with a shrug.

"Please try to remember," Carly said. "Was there anyone at that funeral—a woman—who seemed especially distraught, in the same kind of despair as Valerie had been yesterday?"

Carly caught a glance from Lyle, who probably wondered just why she was asking this question. She wasn't quite sure of that herself.

The pastor's brow crinkled.

"Not especially," he said. "I mean, there were a good many more people at that funeral than the other, and a good many of them were distraught and weeping. Not to be crass, but the emotions were nothing unusual. No one stood out to me."

Is he lying?

Try as she might, Carly couldn't read the man. Neither his face nor his body language gave her any clue as to his honesty.

Lyle crossed his arms and stared at the man skeptically.

"Do you remember any quarrels or altercations during either of the funerals?" he asked. "Specifically, did anyone show any hostility toward Valerie Irwin while she was venting her complaints, or afterwards? Were any threats made?"

"No, I don't think so."

"Are you sure?

"I really don't recall anything like that."

A silence fell. Carly knew that Lyle had one more crucial question.

"Can you account for your own whereabouts at the times of the murders?" he finally asked. He told the preacher the dates and times in question.

Lindsay seemed unperturbed by any suggestion that he could possibly be a suspect.

He cradled his fingers together and said, "I am sure that I was here, at home with my wife, on all those occasions. Her name is Jenice. She can vouch for me if you deem it necessary."

At that moment, Mallory's voice again came over the intercom.

"I'm sorry to interrupt, Miles, but Mrs. Phillips is here for her scheduled appointment."

"I'll be right with her," the pastor replied.

Lindsay rose from his chair.

"And now, if you don't have any further questions, I have a grieving widow to console. I'll thank you not to detain me from my duties."

Although Lindsay was standing now, Carly and Lyle remained in their chairs.

Lyle locked gazes with the pastor. There seemed to be a subtle contest of wills between the two men. Carly knew that if Lyle thought it was important, he would keep up his questioning, whether the pastor had an appointment or not.

Finally Lyle got to his feet, and Carly did too.

"Thank you for your time, reverend," Lyle said in a cold voice, handing the pastor a card. "We may need to get back in touch. In the meantime, please contact us if you can think of any information pertinent to the case."

"I'll do that."

Pastor Lindsay sat back down behind his desk and began looking through some papers as Carly and Lyle exited the office.

There was, in fact, an openly weeping elderly woman sitting in the foyer. As the receptionist escorted the woman into the pastor's office, she darted a grim, suspicious glance at Carly and Lyle.

"Those two are hiding something," Lyle growled as he and Carly exited the rectory and headed toward their car. "I'm sure of it."

CHAPTER EIGHTEEN

"Do you think the good pastor is our killer?" Carly asked Lyle as they walked toward the car.

"Do you?"

She stifled a groan of irritation.

There he goes, being Socratic again.

If her partner was so sure that both the pastor and his receptionist were hiding something, why didn't he just explain his thinking? Instead, he was slipping into his questioning mode. She was well aware that he used that to push her to come to her own conclusions.

Even so, Carly was pleased that Lyle seemed to have come out of his recent dark funk.

"I don't think Pastor Lindsay is a murderer," she said.

"So you think he's innocent?"

"Not exactly."

"So what *do* you think? What do you say we give him a polygraph test?"

Carly laughed aloud.

"Now you're just pulling my leg."

"Why so?"

"Well, for one thing, we've got no forensic justification for it. And for another thing …"

She paused and thought for a moment.

"For another thing," she continued, "he's the type of guy who could beat a polygraph test. He's a cold fish, and he doesn't have normal human responses to things like guilt or regret. Truth and lies are pretty much the same as far as he's concerned. He's got no 'baseline' for truth, so there's no way to read him for lies."

"A true sociopath, huh?"

"Exactly. High-functioning, though. And charismatic. He's probably got his congregation wrapped around his little finger. They just think he's full of love and goodwill."

"But you don't think he's a killer."

"Not exactly. Do you?"

Lyle's jaw twisted as he seemed to literally chew on the question.

“Well, I can’t see him cutting anyone’s throat, anyway. That would be beneath his dignity, and he guards that more than anything. He’d never stoop to anything as messy as face-to-face murder. But he’s hiding something from us. Which makes me wonder whether this case is more complicated than we’ve realized.”

“Like maybe he’s some kind of accessory?”

“Maybe. Or maybe something more than that. And whatever his secret is, his receptionist is in on it.”

“Do you think they’re lovers?”

Lyle scoffed noisily as they got into the car.

“Naw, she’s not his type, too old. He’s not exactly a faithful husband, though. My bet is he’s preying on younger and more nubile women in his congregation. Even so, the receptionist is obviously in love with him, and you wouldn’t want to be on the receiving end of her jealousy. And she’d do anything for him, including lie and cover up for him. For that matter, I’ll bet his wife would too, he’s got that kind of mystique. There’d be no point on checking with her about his alibi.”

Lyle turned the key and started the engine.

“Let’s go find a place where we can get some coffee and talk things over,” he said.

Lyle drove until they came upon a fast food restaurant. They drove through the pickup lane and ordered coffee and pastries. There were plenty of empty spaces in the parking lot, and Lyle pulled into one that faced a few scraggly trees.

Not much of a view, Carly thought, *but better than most in this rundown town.*

“What do we do next?” she asked. and they sat there sipping and eating.

Lyle reached for his cellphone.

“First off, I’ve just got to know what’s this guy’s story,” he said.

A few seconds later, Carly and Lyle were on speakerphone with Zack Elsperger, one of Quantico’s top forensic technicians. As Zack began to talk in his unmistakable nasal voice, she could picture his nerdy face with his round, black-rimmed glasses.

“Hey, guys. Where are you calling from?”

“Harmonium, a near-ghost town in western Pennsylvania,” Lyle said.

Zack let out a chortle of understanding.

“Don’t tell me—it’s one of those old mill towns where the factory up and moved elsewhere, leaving the populace high and dry, and houses empty all over the place, and businesses all boarded up."

"You've got it," Lyle said. "Death is the only growing industry here. And the death business has gotten a little out of hand. We're looking for a serial killer."

"As usual. So how can I help nail him?"

Lyle took a long sip of his coffee.

"I'd like you to find out whatever you can about Miles Lindsay, the pastor at Immanuel Lutheran Church here in Harmonium. Specifically, I'm curious about how he likes to spend his money. I want to know about any suspicious payments."

"I'll get right on it," Zack said. "And don't die yourselves, OK? Towns like that can just suck the life right out of you. The depression alone can kill you."

"We'll try to stay in the land of the living, thanks," Lyle said.

The call ended, and Carly and Lyle sat in silence again for a moment.

So far, she thought, *neither anyone in the land of the living nor the land of the dead has been very helpful on this case.*

Finally Lyle said, "That was kind of an interesting question you asked the pastor back there—something about whether any women at the other funeral were in the same despair as Valerie Irwin. You meant Sarah Tooley, of course. We know she was taking her friend's death hard."

"Actually, I wondered how the pastor would react to being asked about it. But he didn't react at all."

"What got you wondering about that?"

Carly swallowed hard. She still wasn't sure quite what to say. In their communications, both of the murdered women had seemed to feel that they were better off dead. That prompted her curiosity, but she couldn't explain it directly to Lyle.

"Just a hunch," she said. "I guess I've got a feeling …"

Her voice faded for a moment as she thought things through.

"I wonder if the killer doesn't think of himself as some kind of angel of mercy. Maybe he seeks out people whose grief seems to be inconsolable, who don't want to live anymore, and decides to put them out of their misery."

Lyle clucked his tongue approvingly.

"That's an interesting theory. It's a damn shame we don't know anything about the first victim, the homeless guy they called 'Slim.' Maybe he was grieving for somebody too, and had given up on life.

Maybe the killer thought he was doing the guy a favor. The question would be how the killer knew about that. Except for the M.O., he seems completely disconnected from the other victims."

Carly leaned toward her partner.

"Lyle, why don't we go have a look at the homeless man's murder scene?"

He squinted skeptically.

"I'm not sure what good that would do. It's not exactly a fresh crime scene. Nobody even thought it was a murder at the time. Everything will be all cleaned up."

Of course Carly knew that was true. But she hoped that she could get some kind of message from the murdered man at the spot where he'd been killed. That sometimes happened, although she could never count it. Her spirit contacts were unpredictable.

"Maybe some of his homeless buddies are still around," Carly said. "When the cops questioned them before, they probably didn't ask the right questions, since they didn't think it was a murder. Maybe we can find something out that they didn't."

"You might be onto something."

Lyle reached for his cellphone again, and in another moment they were connected with Chief Tallarico.

"Tell me you've got a break in the case," Tallarico said in a sour voice.

"We're working on it," Lyle told him.

"Good. Because I'm going crazy here, with the media and all. The mayor has got me talking to the city council and a slew of reporters instead of doing my job. It's all political and a waste of time. I'm sure glad you're on it. What can you tell me?"

"Can you tell us where to find the place where the homeless man was killed?" Lyle asked.

Chief Tallarico let out a grunt of surprise.

"What good would it do you to go there?"

"It's hard to say just yet. Right now we just need to know how to get there."

"OK, then. It's on the edge of the downtown area, under a bridge where Kimball Street crosses over a drainage ditch just west of Second Avenue. But I sure hope this leads somewhere. I can't help but think you've got better things to do with your time. And we need to get this thing over with."

As call ended, Carly looked up the directions to the location. Lyle drove there, and he parked on Kimball Street as close to the bridge as he could get. When they got out and walked over to the bridge, they found a flight of stairs descending into a concrete-paved drainage gully.

They walked down the stairs to the base of the bridge, where a narrow, foul-smelling little stream crept along the trough of a concrete ditch. Even though the sloping banks were littered with garbage and debris, at first the place seemed to be abandoned.

Then they heard a harsh voice.

"What are you doing here?"

They turned and saw a man's head poking out from the open side of a makeshift cardboard shelter. He was wearing a woolen knit cap, his skin was dull and lusterless, and he had a long scraggy beard.

Carly was startled by an intelligent gleam in the vagrant's eye.

When they produced their badges and introduced themselves, the man let out a hoarse but hearty chuckle.

"FBI, huh?" he said. "So somebody figured out that old Slim didn't commit suicide."

CHAPTER NINETEEN

Carly and Lyle exchanged surprised glances as they stepped across the stream toward the tiny cardboard shanty.

This guy must know something firsthand, she realized.

She was sure there had been no official public suggestion that the vagrant's death was a murder. This case had never even been mentioned in connection with the others.

"You're right; he was murdered," Lyle said to the man. "How did you know? Were you here when it happened?"

The vagrant crawled out into the open and sat looking up at them.

"Naw, I was occupied elsewhere. It happened late at night, and night is my foraging time. I'm usually out and about, hitting the dumpster circuit. Must have been quick and quiet, though. The other guys who *were* here slept right through it."

"Other guys?" Carly asked, glancing around the wasteland beneath the bridge.

"There were five of us living down here at the time, including Slim. The other three moved out right after. Got scared they might be next. I mean, people dying isn't anything new, but all that blood really got to them. Me, I don't let that kind of thing worry me much. Whenever my time comes, I'm ready for it. I don't much care how it happens. I've had a full life."

That struck Carly as an odd thing for a homeless man to say, but he certainly sounded as though he meant it.

"They call me Buster, by the way," he added.

"We'd be grateful for your help, Buster," Lyle said. "Tell me more about what happened."

"I got back just after the guys woke up and saw what they saw. They sent me out to find a cop, which I did."

"It was reported a suicide. What made you think otherwise?"

"It just wasn't Slim's style. He was plenty depressed, and he didn't want to live—and who doesn't get that way from time to time? Most of us don't ever act on that feeling. That's what Slim kept telling me, he just didn't have the nerve to kill himself. He kept wishing somebody would put him out of his misery. Well, I guess some angel must have heard him and made his wish come true."

Then he added with a dark chuckle, "The lucky guy."

Carly remembered her own words with a chill.

"I wonder if the killer doesn't think of himself as some kind of angel of mercy."

"Didn't you tell the cops who showed up on the scene you thought it was a murder?" she asked.

"Sure, but they didn't listen. Truth is, they barely questioned any of us, almost like they were trying to act like we weren't here. Nothin' unusual about that either. I guess a murder would've inconvenienced them. So—they decided it was a suicide. They weren't curious about Slim at all."

"Did you catch the name of the officer who interviewed you?" Lyle asked.

"No. But I remember he had an ugly rusty-looking goatee."

"What can you tell us about Slim?" Carly asked.

"Well, he'd been here a month or so. Don't know where he was before. He heard voices, and he talked back to them. Not an uncommon thing in this kind of life. But I never hear them myself. I do get an interesting little hallucination from time to time, but you don't want to know where those come from."

Carly felt her skin crawl. Of course she knew that voices and visions were common with some people in various stages of mental breakdown. Hers had gone on so long and been so helpful that she no longer stopped to question her sanity over them. But sometimes she had to wonder if she was secretly broken, like these guys appeared to be.

She watched Buster more closely as he continued.

"Whoever it was he talked to, he called her Charlene. Charlene this, Charlene that, he kept talking to her that way. Told her he hoped they'd be together soon. But whenever I asked him about her, he just shut me down."

"Any clue as to who she is or where she lives?" Lyle asked.

"Well, like I said, they were his voices, not mine. I didn't hear them, but I got the impression Charlene was someone who'd died."

Again Carly found herself thinking about her own so-called "gift." Was Slim like her somehow? For all she and Lyle knew, he'd actually been talking with Charlene's spirit.

But that wasn't what she and Lyle needed to find out. The most obvious connection was that all three of the victims were grieving. But what did that mean to this case?

Anything at all?

"I don't suppose Slim was his real name," Carly said to him.

"No, I'm sure it wasn't. For that matter, my real name isn't Buster. We never asked each other what our real names were. I guess we were both private that way. The past is past, and some of us would rather leave it behind—including our so-called 'real names.'"

"Mind telling us what *your* real name is?" Lyle said.

The man winked and smiled through dingy teeth.

"Maybe when we get to know each other better," he said.

Again Carly looked around the garbage-strewn area.

"Could you show us where he was killed?"

"Sure," Buster said, pointing across the stream. "It was right over there. I don't think the sanitation guys managed to get all the bloodstains out of the pavement."

Carly stepped across the stream toward the spot. Sure enough, she saw a large irregular pink stain in the concrete. She heard Lyle's voice as he continued asking the homeless man questions.

"Do you know anything at all about Slim's life before he became homeless? I mean, did he ever mention anyone except Charlene?"

"No, I'm pretty sure he didn't …"

The voices of Lyle and Buster began to fade as Carly stepped onto the pink stain and felt a presence rising up inside of her. She felt unsteady on her feet, so she crouched down to look as though she were searching for evidence. Then she closed her eyes.

And once again, she found herself looking at that pyramid of coffins piled up on that ferryboat as the sea breeze blew against her cheeks and seagulls cried out in the air. She remembered how she'd knocked on a coffin lid in her other visions. But this time she was puzzled. There were so many …

Which coffin lid should I knock on?

As if in reply, she heard a man's voice whispering in her mind.

"Psst. Over here."

"Over where?" Carly asked silently.

"Here."

Carly realized the voice was coming from a coffin just to her left.

She bent near the coffin and asked, "Is this Slim?"

"That's what they called me."

"But what was your real name?"

She heard a vague grumbling sound, as if the spirit didn't really know. Carly was hardly surprised. Spirits who appeared in her visions were often confused and didn't always make very good sense. They seemed to be still trying to process exactly what it meant to be dead.

"What're you doin' here?" the voice asked.

"I'm looking for your killer. Do you know who it was?"

"Huh. I wouldn't know. But stay away from him unless you want to die too. You're a young thing, aren't you? Don't despair. You've got no call for it. Don't throw away the rest of your life. I need you to do something else for me, though."

"What's that?"

A small object took form on top of the coffin—a brass medallion on a neck chain. It showed the image of a man wearing a toga and a halo, holding a large cross in one hand and some kind of stringed musical instrument in the other. Letters were engraved around the edges of the medallion, curving above and below the image.

St. Genesius
pray for us

Then the medallion flipped itself over to reveal two engraved letters.

TP

"Are those your initials—TP?" Carly asked.

The spirit grumbled as if the question was irrelevant.

"Just find this, OK? And give it to Lana. Tell her what happened to me."

"Who's Lana? Your wife?"

"Just do what I'm telling you."

The spirit's voice was fading, getting weaker now. Carly felt panicked that she was going to lose this connection before she could find out anything more.

"But I don't know who Lana is. Where can I find her?"

Then the voice hissed a few words.

"I'll show you."

The scene suddenly changed, and Carly found herself standing on a street corner in a quiet residential area. Across the intersection was a comfortable two-story house with a gabled window above a broad porch. On a post on the corner, a pair of street signs showed the location.

Bayard Avenue / 46th Street

"Wait a minute," Carly said. "What about Charlene? Buster said you used to talk to her. Who is she—or was she?"

But the scene dissolved, and she felt the spirit's presence slip away completely. She opened her eyes and found herself looking at the bloodstain on the concrete under the bridge. She heard Lyle's voice.

"So are you gonna tell me your real name now?"

The homeless man let out a chuckle.

"Don't know why it matters. It's been ten years or more since anyone called me by it. But if you must know, it's—or maybe I should say *was*—John Bowden. I don't guess that information's going to do you much good, though."

Carly turned and saw Lyle closing up his notebook.

"No, I don't suppose it will," Lyle said with a sigh. "Thanks for your time, though."

"Glad to oblige. Stop by again. I'll be here—during the days, at least. But if you find me asleep, don't wake me up."

Carly followed Lyle back up the steps.

"Maybe that wasn't a complete bust," Lyle said as they walked. "All three victims were grieving somebody's death—Valerie for her sister, Sarah for her friend, and this 'Slim' guy for someone named Charlene. Maybe we *are* looking for a killer who imagines himself to be on an errand of mercy."

"I think maybe so," Carly said.

Although the truth was, nothing in her vision proved anything one way or another about that assumption. Instead, she had another woman's name, Lana, and the image of a brass medallion that the spirit wanted Carly to find and give to Lana.

But why? Carly wondered.

And how?

Carly and Lyle got into the car, and Lyle started the engine.

"We'd better stop by City Hall and report in to Tallarico. Maybe we can put our heads together and come up with something."

But Carly felt an anxious tingle.

We'd only be wasting our time.

She felt certain that there was something else they needed to do.

She took out her cellphone and found the location of the street corner in her vision. A satellite view revealed a house that looked like the one she'd seen there.

It's a real place. We need to go there. Right now.

But how could she possibly explain that to Lyle?

CHAPTER TWENTY

What could she say?

Carly's head buzzed as she tried to think of some plausible reason for the request she needed to make.

She couldn't just blurt out to Lyle that she'd gotten the address from the spirit of a murdered man. That would have to be part of much longer conversation, one that she had already put off many times. She hoped to bring it up when they weren't in the middle of an investigation. And given Lyle's edgy frame of mind lately, now seemed hardly a good time for it.

Besides, in this case, there was no logical reason to believe that Slim had been a reliable source even when he was alive. Sometimes her visions were wrong, or at least she misinterpreted them, and sometimes following up what she thought she saw led nowhere.

Even so, Carly had a strong feeling that this lead was a good one, and that they shouldn't waste their time going anywhere else. The killer was surely going to strike again soon. The communication from Slim felt important, and in any case, it was the best lead they had.

But there simply was no sensible explanation. She just had to tell Lyle and hope for the best.

"Lyle," she began cautiously, "there's another stop we should make first."

He glanced over at her with surprise.

"What? Where?"

"I want to stop at the corner of Bayard Avenue and 46th Street."

"Why there?'

"I don't know exactly. It's just—it's just a hunch I have."

"A hunch?"

"Yeah."

"You get those a lot."

"I know."

"What do you expect to find there?"

Carly cringed at the impatience in her partner's voice.

Not that I can blame him, she thought.

"I can't explain it," she said. "But I think this is really important."

Lyle fell silent, still driving steadily in their original direction.

Again, Carly checked out the street corner on GPS.

"It won't be a waste of time," she said. "It's only a few blocks off our route to City Hall."

"Can you tell me anything about why this is so important?" Lyle asked sharply.

"We'll see when we get there. Look, I know this sounds crazy—"

"Yeah, it kind of does."

Lyle glanced over at Carly curiously. She knew he was thinking about all the other times her "gut feelings" had paid off. But usually she'd been able to come up some rationale for her hunches. This time she just couldn't do it.

"Tell me how to get there," Lyle finally said with a growl.

Carly gave him directions, and he drove them to the location in sullen silence.

When they arrived at the corner of Bayard and 46th and pulled up at the curb, Carly drew a deep breath of relief. There was the street corner sign, exactly as she had seen it. And there was the house with the porch and the gabled upper window.

It all looked exactly like it had in her vision.

There were similar houses all along this street, and nothing at all about the scene appeared to be dangerous, or even unusual. It was a slightly rundown, but still respectable, neighborhood.

Lyle didn't turn off the engine.

"OK, we came here," he grumbled. "Are you satisfied? Can we head on over to City Hall now?"

She swallowed hard and hesitated.

"We need to talk to whoever lives in that house on the corner," she said timidly.

"Huh?"

Carly stifled an anxious sigh.

"Let's just knock on the door and see who answers."

"Who do you *expect* to answer?"

Carly struggled to think of something, anything sensible, to say. But there was no way to fake it or make something up, as she often did.

"I think the murdered homeless man lived in that house. I think … his wife lives there now."

Lyle stared at her. He seemed at a loss for words.

"Let's just check it out, OK?" Carly asked.

"No, it's not OK. *Why* do you think the man lived there, or his wife does now? If we're going to ring that doorbell and introduce ourselves as FBI agents, you've got to give me some sort of reason first."

A tense silence fell between them.

Finally Lyle spoke.

"Look, suppose I humor you and go along with this. Can't we at least first find out the names of the people who live there, so we don't look like crazy idiots?"

Carly found it to be a reasonable suggestion—certainly more reasonable than what she herself was asking of Lyle. And that information would be easy enough to come by.

Carly called City Hall on her cellphone and asked to speak to someone in city records. When she got the proper employee on the line, she checked out the house number on the porch.

"Could you tell me who lives at 1334 Bayard Avenue?" she asked.

After a moment's wait, the employee said, "That residence is currently owned and occupied by Travis and Lana Patten. They've lived there for 20 years."

Carly thanked the employee and ended the call.

Lyle was glaring at her again.

"So you think Slim's real name was Travis Patten? Which even Buster didn't know? Are you even going to tell me why?"

Carly flashed back to the initials on the back of that brass medallion she'd seen in her vision.

TP

Travis Patten.

The spirit had said she should find it.

"Give it to Lana," the spirit had said. *"Tell her what happened to me."*

It couldn't all be coincidental. She hadn't misinterpreted the dead man's request. Of course this could still be just about Slim's desire to bring some peace to his wife. But it was also possible that someone here could tell them more about the serial killer still very much at large.

She hadn't found the St. Genesius medallion yet, and had no idea where to look for it. So she still couldn't answer Lyle's question about why they were here. Even so, Carly knew she definitely had to go to that house.

"Let's check it out," she said.

"Carly ..."

"Please, Lyle. I need you to trust me."

Another silence fell. Carly could practically feel the frustration building up inside Lyle. His reprieve from that dark funk was clearly over.

"Look, you don't have to come with me," Carly finally told him. "I understand why you don't want to. I'll go over there by myself while you wait right here in the car. If it's nothing, I'll be back in a minute."

But suddenly he turned off the engine and said, "Let's go."

As they got out of the car and walked toward the house, Carly realized that a reckoning was fast coming due. She'd couldn't let Lyle keep wondering about her "hunches" for much longer.

First things first.

She had to follow up on this vision of hers before she even tried to think about anything else. They walked up onto the porch, and Carly rang the doorbell. In a few moments a middle-aged woman answered the door. She was dressed casually and had an open, friendly expression.

"Can I help you?" the woman asked.

"Are you Lana Patten?" Carly asked.

"Yes."

While Lyle normally made the introductions, he was obviously in no mood to do so right now, so it was up to Carly.

Carly took out her badge and said, "I'm Special Agent Carly See with the FBI, and this is my partner, Special Agent Lyle Ramsey. Could you spare us a few minutes to answer some questions?"

Lana Patten squinted at her curiously.

"Well, I—I suppose so," she stammered uncertainly. "Come on inside."

Carly and Lyle followed the woman into a comfortably furnished living room. The well-used sofa was covered with a colorful throw, and a recliner chair looked like it had recently been wiped clean. On the mantel over a large fireplace, a cluster of knickknacks was free of dust.

Lana Patten sat down on the couch, and Carly and Lyle sat facing her in a pair of armchairs. Carly's brain rushed frantically for a moment as she tried to think of how to get this conversation started.

A worried expression crossed the woman's face.

"Does this have something to do with my husband?" she asked.

Carly and Lyle exchanged uneasy glances.

"Is your husband's name Travis?" Carly asked.

Lana Patten nodded.

Lyle put in, "Is he at home?"

"No," the woman said. "He … hasn't been home for a while."

After a short silence, she added in a quavering voice, "You're here to tell me he's … he's dead, aren't you?"

CHAPTER TWENTY ONE

A sudden silence fell over the living room. Carly felt like she was in a movie that had frozen in midframe. Although she knew that only a few seconds were passing, she had time to see Lana Patten's expression flicker from guilt to pain.

She also had time to see how staggered Lyle was by the woman's words. After all, just a few minutes ago he'd been completely skeptical about Carly's insistence on coming here. In spite of his familiarity with her "hunches," this scene must seem inexplicable.

As normal time seemed to kick back in, Carly pushed herself to deal with the situation. She pulled out her cellphone, brought up the police reports of the three murders, including the photos.

She found photos that had been taken in the morgue of the homeless man's face.

"Ms. Patten, I'm afraid you need to prepare yourself for a shock," she said.

Carly walked over to the couch and sat down beside the woman. She held out her phone, showing a particular picture.

"Can you identify this man?" she asked.

Lana Patten choked on a single horrified sob.

"Oh, my God," she said. "I knew this could happen. It's him. It's Travis."

"Ms. Patten, I'm terribly sorry," Carly said.

Lana Patten shuddered for a moment.

"Give me a moment, please," she said. "I need a drink of water."

She got up from the couch and staggered through an archway into the kitchen. Carly started to follow, and then told herself to give the woman some time alone.

As Carly heard the water running, she saw that Lyle was still staring at her. He looked puzzled—but he also looked more than a little angry.

I've kept too much from him too long, Carly thought.

Lana Patten came back with a glass of water in her trembling hands. She sat down beside Carly again, and took a long swallow.

"How did this happen?" she asked hoarsely. "Was it suicide?"

"He was murdered," Carly said.

"When?"

"About a week ago," Carly said. "His was the first of three serial murders. The most recent was last night."

"We're working to stop the killer before he strikes again," Lyle put in.

"And we need your help," Carly added.

"I—I want to help but, I … still don't understand …" Lana stammered, and then her voice faded.

After a short silence, Carly asked, "Ms. Patten, could you tell us how your husband came to be homeless?"

Lana let out a long, despairing sigh.

"My husband was a good man, but very troubled," she said. "He suffered from schizophrenia and frequently heard voices."

Carly flashed back to what Buster had told them about Slim talking to an imaginary person.

"Charlene this, Charlene that, he kept talking to her that way."

That didn't help clear up any questions about Charlene. As a disembodied voice for Travis, she could be imaginary, or she could be a real person that he thought was actually nearby. Carly wanted to know, but she couldn't very well just blurt out that name. Right now she needed to hear what the widow had to say.

"We tried to get help for him, over and over again. Drugs seemed to work from time to time, Thorazine especially. At least the delusions and voices would stop for a while. But he said he didn't like the way the drugs made him feel. He thought they had a dulling effect, and at the same time they made him feel physically restless. I simply couldn't persuade him to keep taking them."

Carly squinted at the woman curiously.

"Ms. Patten, we are under the impression that your husband had been living under that bridge for a month or so."

Lana Patten shook her head miserably.

"Oh, he'd been gone for longer than that. This time he went away in May, I believe."

This time?

"I'm not sure I understand," Lyle said. "He was missing for more than four months? But he wasn't all that far away. Couldn't the police find him during all that time?"

"I didn't report him missing. I know that sounds terrible, but …"

Her voice faded again, then she continued.

"Travis is—he *was*—a successful CPA. Which of course meant he did most of his work around tax season. Then when May or June came around, he always got restless and uneasy and bored, and sometimes he seemed to think someone somewhere was calling for him, and he wanted to go away."

Lana breathed in slowly.

"The first time he disappeared was five years ago," she said. "I called the police right away, and they found him living in Vernon Park. He was beyond furious when they brought him home. He insisted he hadn't left for good, he'd just wanted to get away for a while, and I had no business interfering in that part of his life."

Lana scoffed.

"Well, I got angry myself when he told me that. We almost got divorced right then and there. Then the next May the same thing happened, and I called the police again, and this time they found him in an alley downtown. And again we had a terrible fight about it, and it almost ended our marriage. But after that …"

Lana shrugged guiltily.

"Of course I knew what he was doing was dangerous. I seriously thought about having him committed. But I couldn't bring myself to do that to him. His dignity and freedom were too precious to him. I let him have his way. I didn't report him missing."

That explains the flicker of guilt, Carly thought.

After all, if she'd reported him missing, maybe he'd still be alive.

But Carly found herself wondering—would she have made the same choice if she'd been in Lana Patten's situation?

I might, she thought, considering the alternative of having a loved one involuntarily institutionalized. *I just might.*

But she was pretty sure Lyle wouldn't.

"I spent whole summers worried sick about him," Lana continued. "But whenever he came back before, he seemed himself again, refreshed and cheerful, like the man I first fell in love with. He was perfectly rational and kind. And he'd actually tell me stories about the adventures he'd had while he'd been away. Last summer he said he'd gone 'on the rails' as a railroad hobo. He'd found that especially exciting."

Lana let out a long sigh of despair.

"This summer I had a very bad feeling about his going away. And now the thing I'd feared worst … has happened."

A sob arose in her throat, and tears streaked her cheeks. Carly gave her a handkerchief and touched her on the shoulder, waiting until she was calm enough to answer more questions.

She saw that Lyle seemed both confused and angry, looking back and forth between Carly and the grieving woman. He was obviously trying to make sense of what he was hearing, and at the same time also resenting Carly's long-held secretiveness more and more with every passing moment.

By the time Lana regained her composure, a different question was tugging at Carly's mind.

"Ms. Patten, this might seem to be an odd thing to ask," she began. "But was your husband … grieving over the loss of someone who had meant a lot to him?"

Lana Patten's red and puffy eyes widened.

"Why, yes. How would you know to ask a thing like that?"

"Please tell us about it," Carly insisted.

"Back in February, his sister committed suicide. You see, mental problems ran in his family. It seemed to be hereditary. His father was chronically depressed, and his mother killed herself when Travis was still a teenager."

"What was his sister's name?" Carly asked.

"Charlene," the woman said. "Charlene Patten."

Carly saw Lyle's expression of amazement as he silently mouthed that name …

"Charlene."

CHAPTER TWENTY TWO

Lyle felt stunned.

Charlene! he thought, turning the name over in his mind.

Just a little while ago, Buster had told them that Slim often spoke to someone "imaginary" named Charlene.

But now it seemed that Charlene was quite real.

And now we know for sure that all the victims were grieving, he realized.

And that was a key bit of information they'd been missing so far. Until this moment he'd felt excluded from Carly's strange line of questioning. But now his own head was filled with questions.

"Ms. Patten, did Charlene have a funeral service?" he asked.

"Yes, she did. Travis and I both attended."

"Where was it held?" Lyle asked.

"Grace Methodist Church."

"And who conducted the service?" Lyle asked.

Lana Patten tilted her head thoughtfully.

"I'm pretty sure it was the regular pastor at the church. Reverend Pugh, I believe his name was."

"Do you remember whether either you or your husband ever had any contact with Pastor Miles Lindsay at the Immanuel Lutheran Church?" Lyle asked.

"Not that I recall."

Lyle felt a slight flash of disappointment. This was the first hint he and Carly had gotten that Pastor Lindsay might not be their prime suspect. Still, Lyle figured it was too early to rule him out. Lindsay might still have had some sort of communication with Travis Patten without his wife knowing about it.

Carly spoke hesitatingly

"Could you tell us … what your husband's demeanor was during the service?"

"I—I'm not sure why it matters."

"It might help for us to know," Carly insisted gently.

Lana's voice choked at the memory.

"He was distraught—very distraught. He spoke at the service, and it caused us all a lot of alarm. He said life wasn't worth living now that Charlene was gone. He said he'd kill himself if he only had the courage."

Lana dabbed her face and added, "Well, as his wife, you can imagine I was very upset about that."

Lyle saw a strange expression cross Carly's face before she spoke again.

"Ms. Patten, would you say your husband was a … religious man?"

Why is she asking that? he wondered.

Lana Patten also looked a bit surprised.

"Well, he wasn't a regular churchgoer, if that's what you mean. Neither was I. And he never talked about religion much, but …"

The woman thought for a moment.

"He did pray from time to time, at least in his way," she said. "He felt a certain kinship to a particular figure—St. Genesius."

Lyle saw Carly trying to suppress a gasp. This bit of information was clearly significant to her.

But why?

What hadn't she told him?

"That went back to his youth," Lana Patten continued. "Before he became a CPA, he wanted to be an actor. And St. Genesius is the patron saint of actors. Before a performance, some actors say, 'St. Genesius, pray for us.' Travis kept saying that all through his life."

Then she leaned forward a little and said, "Now that I think of it, he had a St. Genesius medallion that he always wore around his neck—and I do mean always. Surely he had it on when he died. Was it among his effects? If it was, I'd like to have it, please."

"We'll look into it," Lyle put in.

But something about Carly's expression told him it wasn't going to be that simple.

"Could you … describe the medal for us?" Carly asked.

Lyle was puzzled.

We know it's a St. Genesius medal, he thought. *Isn't that enough?*

The woman also seemed to find that an odd question. It took her a few moments to answer.

"Well, it's made of brass," she said. "It has an engraving on the front of St. Genesius holding a lute in one hand and a cross in the other, and letters that say 'St. Genesius, pray for us.'"

"Anything else?" Carly asked. "Is there anything on the other side?"

The woman's swollen eyes lit up a little.

"Now that I think of it," she said. "It has his initials on the back—TP."

Carly nodded slowly.

"My partner and I will alert the proper people to be sure that you receive any effects he had at the time of his death," Carly said. "As I understand it, his body is still being kept pending identification."

"That's good," Lana said. "But—I know this might seem odd, but I don't care about his body as much as I do about that medallion. There's … more of him still in it, I suppose."

Lyle knew he ought to have other questions for the widow. But this whole mind-boggling episode had come as a surprise to him. His thoughts were becoming a blur.

Fortunately, his partner seemed to be satisfied with what she'd learned from Lana Patten.

"That's all we need for now, Ms. Patten," Carly said, rising from the couch and handing the woman a card. "Please contact us if you remember anything you think we should know."

"I will," the woman said, starting to rise from the couch.

"There's no need to get up," Carly said. "We'll show ourselves out. And again, we're very sorry for your loss."

"Thank you," Lana Patten said, still sitting.

Lyle felt his agitation rise as they left the house. It didn't help that he still felt the effects of the pills he'd taken last night, so much more than the recommended dosage. They'd left him with a headache—and at the same time, a deep urge to see if more of them would settle his nerves.

He wasn't finding it easy to resist that pull.

He and Carly got into their vehicle and sat there in silence for a moment.

When Lyle did speak, he was alarmed to hear his own voice rumble with anger.

"You seem to be taking the lead in this case. So tell me—what should we do now?"

Carly turned toward him with a hurt expression.

"You sound like you're mad at me," she said.

"Shouldn't I be? Carly, I've got no idea where and how you're getting these hints of yours. It's more than just ordinary intuition. How could you possibly have known the victim's widow lived at this address? And what's this business about the medallion? It means something, doesn't it? Are you going to tell me what it is, or are you going to leave me guessing?"

Carly sat staring at the dashboard. Lyle felt his voice shaking now.

"This has gone on too long, Carly. Ever since we've been partners, you keep coming up with crazy hunches and insights. Some of them turn out to be wrong, but more often they turn out to be right. And that's what makes me crazy. Usually you come up with some kind of lame rational explanation for your hunches, and I try my damnedest to believe you, but this time …"

Lyle let out a sharp exhalation of anger.

"This time you're not even trying to make logical sense. We've hit an impasse, Carly. You know as well as I do, it's been coming on for a long time. It's time for you to tell me the truth about yourself."

"What do you think that is?" she asked in a whisper. "The truth about myself, I mean. Surely you've got some ideas about it."

Lyle struggled to bring his breathing under control.

"I think you've got some kind of … weirdness. I think you see and hear things normal people don't see and hear."

A silence fell between them.

"Well, am I right to think that, or am I crazy?" Lyle asked.

"You're not crazy."

"Then tell me about it. You've kept me in the dark too long."

He waited impatiently while Carly took a long, slow breath.

"Lyle, there's so much you don't know, and I don't know where to start, and …"

She fell silent for a moment, then added, "Now isn't the time."

Lyle scoffed noisily.

"Then when *is* the time? Carly, we're partners. We're supposed to trust each other. Don't you think I can deal with the truth?"

He was startled by the sudden sharpness in Carly's voice.

"I don't know, Lyle. Right now, I don't know what you can deal with. Take a good look at yourself, how you've been acting. Something hasn't been right with you ever since we started this case. So am I the only one keeping secrets?"

Lyle stared at her for a moment.

"Are you still worried I went out for a drink last night?" he said.

"Well, did you?"

"No."

"Well, you did *something* last night you're not telling me about. It doesn't take any kind of psychic ability to figure that out. I think you'd better tell me what's going on."

Lyle felt his face heat up with shame. Carly was right, of course, and there was nothing freaky or weird about her catching on to that. He hadn't told her about the pills, and as his partner, she had every right to know.

"Maybe this really isn't the time," he said quietly.

"Or maybe it is. You've never talked to me about what happened to Dawn. You've never opened up about how it affected you—or how it affects us both as partners. I'm scared to death that …"

Carly hesitated for a moment, then added, "I'm scared you're going to hurt yourself."

Lyle felt as though he'd been slapped.

She's right to worry, he realized.

He had to face facts—for the last couple of days, he'd been slipping into self-destructive behavior. He'd spent years trying to put those tendencies behind him, but here he was again. It wasn't fair to keep that to himself.

But now really isn't the time.

"We'll talk later," he said in a chastened voice as he started the car engine. "Right now we've got a case to solve. Let's keep our heads in the game."

He pulled away from the curb and started to drive.

"Let's go to City Hall and check in with Chief Tallarico," he said. "We've got a lot of stuff to sort out with him."

Neither Carly nor Lyle said another word during the drive across Harmonium. But Lyle found himself flashing back to two awful moments—when Dawn had lay there dying at his feet, and when he himself had been helplessly paralyzed and unable to save Carly's life. He felt his body shudder deep down inside.

Getting his head in the game wasn't going to be easy.

Maybe I really shouldn't have taken this case.

But he was in the middle of it now, and he saw no choice but to see it through.

He really wished he could swallow one more of those pills, though.

When they arrived at City Hall, Lyle and Carly headed straight for the wing of the building that served as a police station. As they walked through the desk area bustling with officers and detectives toward Chief Tallarico's glass-enclosed office, Lyle played out in his mind what to tell the chief.

Obviously, he needed to know they'd found the homeless victim's widow and had interviewed her. He also needed to be told that all three of the victims had been grieving over someone's death, and at least two of them had spoken openly about their grief at funeral services.

Grief is what ties them together, Lyle thought.

Maybe Tallarico could help them figure out what that had to do with the murders.

Lyle was just outside Tallarico's office when he noticed that Carly was no longer walking alongside of him. He turned around and saw his partner lagging back, staring at a cop sitting at one of the desks. The cop looked uneasy under Carly's gaze and slammed a desk drawer shut.

"Carly, come on," Lyle said, just loudly enough to be heard over the din of the room.

Carly turned toward him and followed him into the chief's office.

"Tell me you've gotten a break in the case," the chief said, rising from his chair. "I could really use some good news right now."

Before Lyle could say anything, Carly spoke up, pointing outside the office.

"Who is that cop sitting at that desk?" she asked.

Tallarico looked surprised at the question.

"Why, that's Ross Campbell," he said. "Why do you ask?"

"Does he have any connection to the serial case?"

"As a matter of fact he does," Tallarico said. "He was one of the officers on the scene of the homeless man's murder. I may have mentioned him before. It's probably thanks to him we even figured out we were dealing with a serial killer. He noticed the penny next to the homeless man's body, then later figured out that it had something to do with the penny in Sarah Tooley's hand."

Lyle could see hesitation in Carly's face.

"You've got a problem with him," she finally said to Tallarico.

CHAPTER TWENTY THREE

Carly held her breath as she waited for Chief Tallarico to respond.

Give him a moment, she thought.

After all, she'd just cast suspicion on one of his own cops. That could be more than a bit of a bombshell. She actually wished she hadn't spoken up so quickly. She was afraid she wasn't at her best after her quarrel with Lyle just now.

"What do you mean?" Tallarico said a bit sharply but with a noticeable lack of surprise. "Has it got something to do with why you wanted to go see the homeless guy's murder scene?"

"We did go down under that bridge," Carly told him. "We talked to one of the victim's buddies. We found out that the victim's real name was Travis Patten. We paid his wife a visit. She gave us some information that could turn out to be important."

"Such as?"

"She described a brass St. Genesius medal that the victim always wore."

"So?"

"I believe it may have been stolen after he died."

"That wouldn't be unusual. Especially in a location like that."

Carly was grateful that she didn't have to figure out how to avoid admitting she'd seen the medallion while communicating with a dead spirit. This time she actually had a description of the same item from a living human.

"When I walked past Officer Campbell's desk, I saw that he had exactly that kind of medal on his key ring. When he noticed me looking at it, he tucked it away in his desk drawer. The bottom one on the right."

"Must be lots of people who have a medal like that," Tallarico said with a skeptical shake of his head.

"I know," Carly said. "But according to the widow, this one would have the murdered man's initials engraved on the back—TP."

Again, Carly observed that the chief wasn't as surprised as she'd expected.

Tallarico shook his head slowly and muttered almost inaudibly.

"I knew there was something wrong with Campbell."

He stood up from his desk and walked right past Carly and Lyle and out of his office.

They followed him to the desk where the officer in question was occupied with paperwork. Now that Carly looked again at Campbell, she remembered Buster's description of the cop who had interviewed him.

"He had an ugly rusty-looking goatee."

This was the same guy, all right. He had an unruly tuft of rust-red hair on his chin, and his face seemed to settle naturally into an insolent expression. Carly took an instant dislike to him—a dislike that Tallarico apparently shared.

As Tallarico approached him, the man at the desk looked up with a slight sneer.

"What can I do for you, chief?" he asked.

"I want a look at your key ring," Tallarico said, holding out his hand.

Campbell's heavy eyebrows lowered ominously.

He gave Carly a baleful stare.

She could practically see his mind churning with questions about what Carly knew and what she might have told the chief about that key ring.

Then the cop's sneer sharpened into a smirk.

"What for?" he asked Tallarico.

"It doesn't matter what for," Tallarico replied sharply. "Just show it to me."

Campbell leaned back in his swivel chair and chuckled snidely.

"Well, I can't do that at the moment, chief."

"Why not?"

"Because as it happens, I misplaced my keys a while ago. Been looking all over the station them. I'm worried sick about them, to tell you the truth. So it's funny you should ask about them."

He pulled his desk's pencil drawer open, revealing a clutter of note pads, writing utensils, candy bars, and empty wrappers. Then he put his hands behind his head and swiveled back and forth.

"See, no keys. If you find them, let me know, OK?"

He struck Carly as not only arrogant but remarkably puerile, like a high school punk called into the principal's office.

"I know where you can find your damn keys," Tallarico growled. "Try the bottom drawer on the right."

Campbell's seemingly perpetual sneer faded a little.

"I already looked there," he said.

"Look again."

Campbell was doing his best to intimidate the chief with his stare. Carly guessed it was a tactic that worked on a lot of people, but apparently not on Tallarico.

"Later," Campbell said, waving his hand over his paperwork. "As you can see, I'm kind of busy right now."

"Don't play games with me, Campbell."

"Who's playing games?" Campbell said, tossing Carly a contemptuous glance. "What did this FBI lady tell you about me, anyway? You know how these Feds are. When a case gets the better of them, they figure out some way to meddle with the locals so people don't notice how incompetent they are. They just make stuff up."

Carly noticed that the officers at the surrounding desks had paused in their activities to watch the unfolding scene with interest. She had a feeling that some of them knew how this episode was going to end and were looking forward to seeing it play out.

Tallarico crossed his arms.

"Open the drawer, Campbell," he said.

As if mirroring Tallarico, Campbell crossed his arms.

"I don't think I will, chief," he said. "I mean, what's my keychain to you, anyway? What do you care about it? The least you could do is tell me what this is all about. But even if you did, you can't make me open that drawer. Those contents are personal, and you've got no business seeing them. I've got a right to privacy."

Tallarico let out a snort of disgust.

"Not in this office, you don't," he said. "You're a city employee, and I'm your superior, and you've got no privacy rights here. The contents of your desk are an open book."

"I'll bet a lawyer would disagree."

"Bring it on," Tallarico snapped.

And with a single abrupt but deft movement, Tallarico shoved Campbell in the chest, sending his chair rolling backwards a couple of feet away from the desk.

"Hey, that's assault," Campbell said.

"Oh, did I hurt you?" Tallarico said in a sarcastic cooing voice. "Poor little thing."

The chief leaned over and yanked the bottom right desk drawer open to reveal a peculiar collection of objects, including a college class ring, a plastic whistle, a pair of silver cufflinks, a military medal, a small rubber duck, an inexpensive wristwatch, a gold locket, and a pink-dyed lucky rabbit's foot one might win as a carnival prize. Some of the objects looked like they might be valuable; some were obviously worthless. And of course, a keychain was visible there as well.

"You son of a bitch," Tallarico growled.

For a moment, he seemed especially interested in the rubber duck, which he picked up and examined silently while Campbell squirmed in his seat.

Then the chief dropped the duck back into the drawer. He snapped up the keychain and tossed it to Carly.

"Is this what we're looking for?"

On it hung a small St. Genesius medallion.

Carly was momentarily startled by how precisely the medallion resembled the one she'd seen in her vision, including the inscription surrounding the engraved image of the saint.

St. Genesius
pray for us

She flipped it over, and sure enough she found the engraved letters.

TP

"This is it," Carly said with a nod. "This belonged to the murdered man."

A silence fell over the once-bustling work area.

What happens now? she wondered.

Things were happening too quickly for her to think them through. Just how damning was this bit of evidence? And why had the collection of objects provoked Chief Tallarico's ire?

Especially the rubber duck?

Chief Tallarico pointed to the officer at the nearest desk.

"Sanchez, do you have a pair of cuffs handy?"

The cop nodded dumbly.

"Good," Tallarico growled. "I want you to put Campbell here under arrest."

CHAPTER TWENTY FOUR

The entire room went silent.

Is this case over? Carly was wondering.

She couldn't quite believe that. The medallion theft alone seemed like much too slender a piece of evidence. And so far nothing tied this cop to the other two murders. But maybe there was something they didn't know yet.

We need to talk to this guy, she thought.

In any case, it was obvious that Chief Tallarico was going to make an arrest right here and now.

Just a few moments ago the desk area had been lively with officers and detectives exchanging information or banter. Now everything was suddenly still. And Officer Sanchez hadn't yet obeyed Tallarico's order.

Carly thought that Sanchez actually trembled a little when his eyes met Campbell's. It looked like Sanchez was trying to decide who intimidated him more—Campbell or the police chief. Most of the other cops in the room seemed to be waiting to see how that turned out.

Chief Tallarico himself did not appear at all intimidated.

"Did you hear me, Sanchez?" he barked.

Sanchez nodded again.

"Then do what I told you to do."

Sanchez stammered, "But sir, Campbell is … he's …"

Campbell snapped sarcastically, "Yeah, yeah, a brother officer, I get it. Arrest him anyway—or you'll be next."

Sanchez shrugged and took out his cuffs and walked toward Campbell, who was on his feet now. Campbell put his hands behind his back with a contemptuous grin.

"Ross, I'm really sorry …" Sanchez murmured, getting his cuffs ready.

"Just following orders, right?" Campbell sneered at him. "Always got to obey 'the man,' don't we? Don't worry, I won't take it personal."

Sanchez began to recite the Miranda rights as he put the cuffs on his colleague.

"Oh, shut up, Sanchez," Campbell grumbled.

"You just keep right on, Sanchez," Chief Tallarico countered. "I want this arrest to be airtight and by the book. And let me know the minute he's properly booked and in a holding cell and available for questioning. I want to do that right away."

Campbell gave the chief a defiant look.

"In a hurry, are you, chief?" he snarled. "Scared of me lawyering up? You ought to be. I'll have a lawyer before you can snap your fingers, and you know who he's going to be. I'm going to sue your butt from here to Kingdom Come."

"Like I said before, bring it on," Tallarico said.

As Sanchez escorted Campbell out the door, Carly and Lyle followed Tallarico back into his office, where he dropped heavily into his chair and began drumming his fingers on the desktop. They again took their seats in front of the desk.

"I wish I could say I was surprised," Tallarico muttered. "That creep Campbell is no damn good."

"Uh, my partner and I are a little lost here," Lyle said. "Maybe you could explain a few things."

Tallarico let out a groan of frustration.

"We've been getting reports for a year and a half now about items stolen from homeless people. Sometimes homeless guys complain they've been robbed in their sleep. Sometimes their families notice something missing from their belongings when they identify their bodies after they die."

Like a St. Genesius medallion, Carly realized.

She remembered Lana Patten asking about it.

"Was it among his effects? If it was, I'd like to have it, please."

"The homeless people always thought a cop was robbing them," Tallarico continued. "As much as I hated to think that, I couldn't shake off a hunch that they were right. But I've never been able to prove it—until now."

"So those trinkets in Campbell's desk …" Carly began.

"I recognized some of them as reported missing items. That little rubber duck, for example. After an old man died over in Vernon Park, his grandson said he ought to have had it on him. He'd kept it as a good luck charm, he'd said, and he hung onto it for dear life. Well, now we know who the thief was. Campbell was collecting all that stuff as trophies. Or maybe some of them even to sell."

Carly felt a queasiness in the pit of her stomach. Could anything be creepier than stealing from homeless people?

Of course, the answer to that question immediately dawned on her.

Cutting people's throats was even creepier.

Are we dealing with a man who does both? she wondered.

Had he cut the vagrant and enjoyed it so much that he went on to others? She didn't think that connection quite held up. As far as they knew, nothing had been missing from the other two crime scenes. And it seemed to her that something more than pleasure was motivating this killer.

Lyle scratched his chin as he took in what he was hearing.

"Tell us more about Campbell," he said to Tallarico.

"The truth is, he's a good cop. At least he gets the job done. He's smart and efficient. But he's got this, uh, kind of macho charisma, and he's got one hell of an ego, and he has an unhealthy influence on the rest of the officers. He's sort of their 'alpha male,' so to speak. He sometimes positively enjoys undermining my authority."

"Do you think Campbell is capable of murder?" Lyle asked the police chief.

"I don't know. You're the profilers. Maybe you can tell me."

Silence fell as the three of them struggled with their thoughts. But before Carly and her colleague could contribute anything, Mayor Freelander came storming into the office.

"I just heard the news," the rotund man said breathlessly. "Is it true you've made an arrest?"

For a moment Carly was surprised at how quickly word had reached the mayor, and how quickly he had arrived here. But she reminded herself how the City Hall building was packed full of departments and services all connected with interior hallways, including the mayor's office.

Someone here in the police area had surely called Freelander right away to tell him what had happened. Judging from how he was sweating, Carly guessed that the mayor had jogged his way through those halls.

"Yeah, we've made an arrest," the chief said without rising from his chair.

"Is it true the suspect is a cop?" the mayor demanded, pacing back and forth.

Lyle spoke up in a cautionary tone.

"We need to go easy on the 'suspect' talk. The case isn't exactly closed."

"That's right," Tallarico explained. "We've arrested Officer

Campbell for stealing belongings from homeless people."

The mayor's brow crinkled warily.

"What does that have to do with the murders?"

"That's what we're trying to determine," Tallarico said. "Maybe nothing, maybe everything. One of the homeless men he stole from was the first of the three victims—the man under the bridge. We caught him red-handed with a medallion he apparently snatched off the dead man's body."

Freelander's eyes lit up anew.

"Well, that cinches things, doesn't it? It can't be just a coincidence that your man stole from one of the victims, can it? He's got to be the killer. So you've just about got the case wrapped up with a nice little bow."

Carly suppressed a sigh of her own. She was sure that she and Lyle and Tallarico were thinking the same thing. Things were suddenly moving along very fast, and right now it could be dangerous for them to get overly confident.

It might not be that simple.

At that moment, Officer Sanchez knocked on the door and stuck his head inside.

"We've got Campbell booked and ready. He's on his way to the interrogation room right now."

Tallarico jumped out of his chair.

"Let's go have a little chat with him," he said to Carly and Lyle.

"I'll join you," the mayor said.

"Now wait a minute, Ike—" Tallarico started to protest.

"Don't argue, Vince," Freelander replied. "I've got every right. It was my idea to bring in the FBI. You didn't even want them. But I was right, wasn't I? If it weren't for me, you wouldn't have caught the killer. I deserve to be kept in the loop."

"But we're not even sure—"

"I'll stay out of the way. I'll watch and listen behind the one-way mirror. It'll be like I'm not even there."

Tallarico shook his head with a growl of resignation.

"OK," he said, rising from his desk. "Let's get going."

Tallarico headed out of the office with the mayor right on his heels and Lyle and Carly close behind them. Meanwhile, Carly felt dazed by this turn of events. Was it possible they'd already caught the killer?

She wanted to hope so, but things were moving so fast …

I've got a bad feeling about this arrest.

CHAPTER TWENTY FIVE

Carly's spirits sank.

Looking through the one-way mirror from the booth outside the interview room, she could see that the just-arrested cop wasn't alone in there. Reinforcements had already arrived.

Cuffed and still in uniform, Officer Campbell was seated at the battleship-gray table in a pale gray room. Sitting beside him was a slim man in a business suit who was jotting down notes on a legal pad.

Carly remembered Campbell telling Tallarico he was going to lawyer up *"before you can snap your fingers."*

He wasn't kidding, she thought. *That was incredibly fast.*

At Tallarico's signal, both she and Lyle followed him into the interview room. The mayor stayed behind in the booth, watching through the mirror. Carly was glad of that, because the space inside the little room was uncomfortably tight even for so few people.

At least there were enough chairs. The three of them shuffled around and seated themselves on the opposite side of the table from the two men who awaited them.

The lawyer was middle-aged and cleanshaven with a reasonably fresh haircut, but with a heavily pock-mocked face. His suit and tie appeared a little outdated, but not as worn-out looking as many she'd seen here in the City Hall complex.

The man looked up from his legal pad.

"I've got to say, Vince, I never thought I'd be sitting across this table from you," he said.

"Feels weird, doesn't it?" Tallarico replied sourly.

Neither man seemed at all comfortable with the situation. Carly assumed that they had a long history together—and this was probably the first time they'd found themselves on opposite sides.

Tallarico then made introductions.

"Agents See and Ramsey, this is Kevin Dench, the lawyer who usually represents my guys when police misconduct cases come up. Kevin, these are Special Agents Ramsey and See of the FBI."

"FBI, huh?" Dench replied with a scoff. "Pretty hardcore. Isn't that kind over overkill for the case at hand?"

“Not if your client is guilty of murder.”

“Murder!”

Dench seemed startled. Apparently his client hadn’t described the possible charges in any detail.

“What are you thinking, anyway?” the lawyer asked, looking back and forth at the three faces across from him. “FBI? So this is about the current run of serial killings? You must be crazy if you think my client had anything to do with that.”

“Let’s start small,” Tallarico said, staring hard at Campbell. “What were you doing with stolen items in your desk drawer?”

Dench began, “My client’s not going to answer—”

But Campbell interrupted him.

“I don’t know anything about them. I’d never seen them until you yanked that drawer open. Somebody must have put them there when I wasn’t around.”

Leaning across the table toward Tallarico he added, “I wonder who would’ve done anything like that.”

“Officer Campbell, I strongly advise—” Dench began.

But Campbell interrupted him again.

“Yeah, yeah, I know, I’ve got a right not to incriminate myself. But since I’m innocent, that’s not gonna happen. I didn’t steal anything from anybody, and everybody here knows it.”

At that point, Carly was tempted to enter the fray with what she knew about the St. Genesius medal. The dead vagrant’s treasured belonging had turned up on Officer Campbell’s personal keychain.

But the lawyer stated firmly, “This interview is over.”

“No, it’s not,” Campbell objected. “I want to make it known, I’m the aggrieved party here. The chief here has had it in for me for a long time. He’ll do just about anything to bust me. How about an illegal search? How about planting evidence? And oh, hey, how about assault?”

Jabbing his finger at the police chief, he hissed, “Did I happen to mention Tallarico here physically attacked me?”

Before Tallarico could protest, Dench spoke more sharply than before.

“Officer Campbell, do you want my representation or not?”

Campbell hunched over indignantly and fell silent.

“Like I said,” Dench snapped, putting his legal pad into his briefcase, “this interview is over. Let’s get out of here, Officer Campbell.”

When Campbell seemed about to balk, Dench stood up and added, "Right now. Or you're on your own."

Still grumbling, Campbell got to his feet too.

But before the two could leave, the door to the room swung open.

"Not so fast," a familiar voice cried. "I've got a few questions of my own."

Dench's eyes widened with surprise, and Campbell let out a hearty chuckle.

"Wow, first the FBI, and now Mayor Freelander," Campbell said. "Talk about big guns. I could get an exaggerated notion of my own importance."

I think that ship has already sailed, Carly thought.

The mayor was standing the doorway now, doing his best to block Campbell and Dench's exit.

"You've got a hell of a lot to answer for, officer," he said, shoving Campbell in the chest.

Campbell was laughing heartily now.

"Hey, do you see this?" he said to his lawyer. "Now the *mayor* is assaulting me! I'm going to sue this city until its coffers are dry! 'Course, that probably won't be too long, the way this town is going downhill."

"I didn't assault you and you know it," the mayor said.

"Like hell you didn't," Campbell said. "I've got three witnesses."

Campbell sneered at Carly, Lyle, and Tallarico.

"Unless you guys plan to perjure yourselves," he added. "I wouldn't put it past you. It's a fine day when law enforcement people won't stand up for their own."

The mayor's face had turned bright red.

"Your murderous antics have put the whole future of Harmonium in jeopardy," he said.

Campbell chuckled some more.

"Well, it's nice to know your priorities, Mr. Mayor. To hell with people's safety. What matters to you is 'the future of Harmonium'—real estate, business, urban renewal, whatever it takes to grease your palm."

"Are you accusing me of corruption?"

"Hey, did I say that? But if the shoe fits …"

The room rang with a shout from Dench.

"That's enough! Both of you!"

Carly was on the verge of breaking out in laughter at the sheer absurdity of the scene. She'd never seen a defense lawyer lose his cool at both his client and a city's top-ranking official before.

Dench took a deep breath, trying recover his poise.

"Let's get you back to your holding cell," he said, grabbing Campbell by the arm and pushing him past the mayor.

"I'm not finished talking to you," Mayor Freelander snarled, starting to follow the two men out of the interview room. Then he stopped and turned back toward Carly, Lyle, and Chief Tallarico.

"By the way … great work, you guys. I'll be sure to give you all due credit when I announce this to the media shortly."

"Announce *what?"* Tallarico asked with a note of alarm.

"That we've got the killer in custody, of course."

"Ike, hold on just a minute—" Tallarico began.

"Of course, I'm sure See and Ramsey are eager to get back to Quantico. Have a good trip, folks."

The mayor strode out of the room and shut the door behind him. Silence fell in the room—and Carly found it a welcome silence after all the turmoil that had just occurred.

Tallarico shook his head.

"Campbell really is a piece of work," he muttered.

Lyle leaned back in his chair and said, "Well, I don't think you'll need to worry about him much longer. Whatever that guy is guilty of, he won't get away with it. He's his own worst enemy, and a defense attorney's worst nightmare. Chances are he'll confess just to hear the sound of his own voice—or at least to avoid too much jail time. And there's no way he's going to get off on account of any so-called assault or illegal search. He'll never be a cop again."

Tallarico heaved a long, discouraged sigh.

"Yeah, but it's a long way from robbing homeless people to slashing folks' throats. Do you think he's our murderer?"

Another silence fell.

"It's not impossible," Lyle finally said. "It wouldn't be the first time a serial killer himself was involved with law enforcement. And if he's arrogant enough, he might have robbed the body and even made sure he was one of first cops at the murder scene, just to prove to himself he could get away with it. But …"

"But what?" Tallarico asked as Lyle's voice faded.

"My partner and I have been trying to develop a profile of the killer, and Campbell doesn't exactly fit it. For one thing, my guess is that this killer is a much cooler character than Campbell. He wouldn't act as recklessly as Campbell did just now. Not in public, not in secret."

"Also," Carly put in, "we don't think that this particular killer acts out of thrills or for the fun of it. We now know that *all* the murder victims were in deep states of mourning. It's likely the killer knew this about them. It's even possible that's why he selected them. He might see it as an act of kindness. He might see himself as an angel of mercy."

"That sure doesn't sound to me like Campbell," Tallarico said.

"I don't guess it does," Lyle said.

The three of them fell silent for a moment. Carly found herself wondering—had anything good come from pursuing this subject.

I can think of one thing, she realized.

"You need to give Travis Patten's effects to his widow, Lana, as soon as you can," she said. "Especially the St. Genesius medallion."

"I'll do that," Tallarico said, jotting down a note to that effect.

Carly felt at least a glimmer of satisfaction. Returning that medallion to Lana Patten was no small kindness. The woman had actually said she cared more about it than she did about her husband's body.

"Do you have any other potential suspects?" Tallarico asked.

"A person of some interest, anyway," Lyle told him. "We know that the same preacher conducted two of the victims' funerals—Reverend Miles Lindsay, pastor at Immanuel Lutheran Church. He didn't preside at the homeless man's funeral, but that doesn't mean he didn't attend it or didn't at least know the man."

"A preacher—a killer?" Tallarico asked.

"We don't think he commits the murders on his own," Carly said. "But he might be connected with them somehow. Maybe he even arranges them."

"But why?"

"Like I said, maybe he considers himself an angel of mercy," Carly said. "Maybe Pastor Lindsay takes his ministrative duties a little too much to heart. Maybe he thinks he should not only comfort his flock, but he should also put some of them out of their sufferings by killing them and sending them on a quick route to heaven."

"Like I said before, this killer himself is no sadist," Lyle reminded Tallarico. "He makes his deaths as quick and painless as possible. Your coroner agreed with me about that."

Tallarico's eyes widened with surprise.

"I've heard of killers who get the mercy bug," he replied. "Usually nurses or hospital staff. They see so much pain and death, they go off the edge. But a preacher would have to be a real psychopath to actually carry out that kind of a plan."

"This killer *is* a psychopath. And like a lot of psychopaths, he probably lives a perfectly respectable life. Nobody around him has any idea how evil he is. He might be highly thought-of in his community, even revered. A preacher might fit that sort of profile."

"Should we go pick him up?" Tallarico asked.

"No, this theory is much too thin for that. But Agent See and I did pay him a visit a while ago, and he set off a few alarms for us. He's got all the marks of a true sociopath. And he was definitely hiding something from us—something illegal, possibly even worse."

"We need to investigate this man," Tallarico said.

"We're already doing that," Carly said. "We've got one of Quantico's top forensic technicians finding out whatever he can about him."

Lyle looked at his watch.

"As a matter of fact, we might want to check in with him and see if he's turned up anything."

Lyle took out his cellphone and put in a call to Zack Elsperger. When Zack picked up the call, Lyle set the phone on the table and put it on speaker.

"Hey, Zack," Lyle said. "This is Lyle Ramsey getting back to you, and I'm here with Carly See. We've also got Harmonium's police chief on the line, Vince Tallarico."

Zack replied in his usual nerdy manner.

"Pleased to meet you, chief. I'm Zack Elsperger, and I'm a technical wizard. Something of a legend, really."

"It's always a pleasure getting to know a legend, Zack," Tallarico said with an amused smile.

"Zack, have you found any info about Pastor Lindsay?" Lyle asked.

Zack let out a satisfied chuckle.

"Well, I'm still working on it—but I've already found something interesting. Really interesting."

CHAPTER TWENTY SIX

The three investigators exchanged eager glances.

Maybe it's the break we need, Carly thought.

"What have you got?" Tallarico asked Zack.

"One of the classics. It seems this Pastor Lindsay of yours sneaks off to casinos whenever he can, including to Vegas, and he loses pretty consistently. He's racked up about a quarter of a million in credit card debts—more than he can hope to pay on a preacher's salary. I suspect he also owes money to one or two loan sharks."

"Quite a gambling problem then," Tallarico said.

The chief's expression had quickened with interest, but Carly noticed that her partner actually looked disappointed.

"Anything else?" Lyle asked.

"Like I said, I'm still working on it," Zack replied. "But it also looks like he's fleecing his flock pretty vigorously, so to speak."

"Embezzling church funds?" Tallarico asked.

"That's right. I'll be able to give you some specifics in the next hour or so."

Lyle cracked his knuckles nervously.

"Did you find anything that looks like payment to a killer-for-hire?" he asked.

"Nope, nothing like that. Seems to be just the old-fashioned compulsion to stimulate the brain's reward system with big wins that hardly ever happen."

"Yeah. I understand that it's an ugly addiction," Tallarico said.

"And some addicts are willing to risk losing everything else for the sake of it," Zack said.

"OK, good work, Zack," Lyle said. "When you find out more, be sure to contact Chief Tallarico."

"I'll do that. Good luck, you guys."

"Thanks," Lyle said, ending the call.

Carly, Lyle, and Tallarico sat looking at each other for a moment. Finally Lyle let out a discouraged sigh.

"Zack's good," he said to Tallarico, "In a little while you'll have enough information to charge Pastor Lindsay for embezzlement. When you do, you'll also want to look into his receptionist, Mallory Butler. Whatever he's up to, she's in on it too. She's definitely an accomplice."

Lyle drummed his fingers on the table and added, "But Lindsay's not the guy we're looking for. He's got nothing to do with the murders."

"How do you know?" Tallarico asked. "If it's like Zack says, and this guy is willing to risk anything …"

Lyle didn't reply, just shook his head wearily. But Carly understood what he meant.

"He doesn't fit the killer profile," she told Tallarico. "He's crooked because he's a gambling addict, but it's all about getting the money to feed his habit and covering it up and keeping up appearances for his congregation. And while some addicts might kill for the sake of their high, Lindsay isn't the type to get mixed up in murder, even indirectly. He might also have affairs with his female parishioners, which is sleazy but not criminal."

"So where does that leave us?" Tallarico said.

"Pretty much nowhere," Lyle said.

Carly thought her partner looked positively punctured. At times earlier today, he'd seemed like his usual self, alert and even brilliant. But something more than a setback in the case seemed to be getting to him.

What's going on? she wondered yet again.

"Meanwhile," Lyle said, "the mayor's in full performance mode, about to make a statement to the media that we've caught the killer. Do you think you can talk him out of it?"

Tallarico scoffed.

"I can try, but he's not gonna listen. You don't know Ike Freelander like I do. He wants this whole thing settled fast. Now that I think about it, that might not be so different from the kind of gambling addiction your research guy was talking about—that thing about using some kind of success to kick in the brain's reward system."

The chief squinted at them and added, "To make matters worse, he thinks the two of you are going to head back to Quantico. And that's his call, really. It was his idea for you to come here, and he put in the request. It's up to him to decide when you should leave. For my part …"

He shrugged and added, "I'd like you to hang around, if that's OK with you."

"We'd be glad to," Carly told him quickly.

"Just try to keep a low profile. And whatever you do, don't let on to Freelander that you're still investigating the case. He hates to be contradicted, especially about things he says in public. And he'd find some way to make your job harder."

Tallarico got up from his chair.

"Anyhow, I'd better go and try to talk sense to him. Not much chance at success though. I hope you have better luck. Keep working, and let me know right away if you get any breaks. We'll need something strong to convince the mayor he's wrong."

Tallarico left the interview room. Carly and Lyle sat there in silence for a long moment. Carly thought Lyle's face looked worn and tired. Something had seemed to be wrong with him ever since yesterday.

I should have pushed back more about his taking this case, she thought. *I should have talked him out of it.*

"What do we do now?" she finally asked.

He looked a little surprised, as though he'd lost track of where they were.

"Let's go somewhere to get something to eat," he said. "I don't know about you, but I'm hungry."

The two of them headed out of the building to their vehicle. But when they got inside, Lyle didn't start the engine. He just sat staring at the dashboard with a vacant expression.

"Lyle, what's wrong?" Carly asked quietly.

Lyle growled under his breath.

"You mean aside from the fact that we're completely stymied, and there's still a serial killer out there planning his next murder, and he's probably laughing at us right this minute? There's nothing wrong. Everything's just peachy."

Carly was shocked by his tone of voice. It wasn't just the note of cruelty and uncharacteristic sarcasm. She heard something else as well.

He sounds frightened, she thought.

"Lyle, we've talked about this before," she said. "Maybe you came back to work too soon. Maybe that trauma you went through on the last case—"

Lyle interrupted sharply.

"Oh, for Pete's sake, Carly, let's not go over this again. I'm fine, OK? There's nothing wrong with me that solving this case won't fix. And anyway, I don't know where you get off questioning my state of mind like this. You're the one who's got some explaining to do."

"What do you mean?"

"You know what I mean. A little while ago you happened to mention you've got some kind of weird psychic abilities. Really? That's quite a thing to unload on me all of a sudden. We've been working together for a long time. Don't you think you might have brought that up before?"

Carly felt stung. She was trying to see things from Lyle's point of view. But wasn't this scene the very kind of thing that kept her from mentioning her strange contacts to anyone at all? Besides, she didn't believe that her psychic abilities were really the biggest issue between them at the moment. Her messages from dead people were not what was really bothering her partner.

There's something else.

Lyle's hands were gripping the steering wheel hard. His body appeared to be trembling. Carly could even hear his teeth grinding.

She couldn't remember ever seeing him in such a state.

"I can't talk to you when you're like this," she said in a whisper.

"Well, that's just too damn bad."

Lyle reached for the keys to turn the ignition. Then his hand visibly shook and dropped onto his thigh. He shuddered from head to foot. He blinked and choked aloud, as if trying to hold back tears.

"Lyle, talk to me," Carly pleaded.

Lyle seemed to be struggling to find the right words to say. He slumped forward, and his forehead almost touched the steering wheel. Then he reached forward and snapped open the trunk of the car.

"I'll be back in a minute," he said curtly, opening the car door.

"Where are you going?" Carly asked.

"Nowhere. I'll be right back. Stay there."

Carly's thoughts went into overdrive, processing a whole series of questions in desperate split-seconds.

What would happen now if she let Lyle get out of the car, to do whatever he wanted to do?

What *did* he want to do?

What's in the car trunk, anyway?

Of course their go-bags were in the trunk. Even when they were staying in local hotels, they kept their go-bags in the car by day in case there was a sudden change in their itinerary …

Something in his go-bag …

It was something he wanted urgently—and he didn't want to tell Carly about it.

Meanwhile, Lyle had stepped out of the car.

“Come back here,” Carly said.

Ignoring her, Lyle closed the car door and headed toward the open trunk.

In a flash, Carly opened her passenger door and scrambled out of the car. She arrived at the half-opened trunk exactly when Lyle did.

Lyle lifted the trunk lid the rest of the way open, but Carly reached for the handle of his go-bag before he could grab it. She pulled the bag out of the trunk and hugged it to keep it away from him.

“What’s in here?”

“N-nothing,” Lyle stammered. “I just wanted to … make sure I didn’t leave anything in the hotel room.”

“What’s in here?” Carly repeated.

She could see Lyle’s jaw twitch.

There was anger in his eyes and he reached to take the bag away from her.

“Never mind. I don’t need to check anything. Everything’s fine.”

But Carly stepped back from him.

“I want you to tell me what’s in here.”

“No.”

“Then open it up and let me see.”

“No.”

“Then I’m going to open it myself.”

Lyle’s eyes widened with shock, and Carly understood why. She’d never said anything like this to him before. She’d never even considered such a thing. They’d always respected each other’s privacy without any question.

Was she going to change all that in a single instant?

Opening the bag might be a breach of trust that could never be forgiven

On the other hand …

He’s my friend. He’s my best friend. Probably the best friend I’ve ever had.

And now he was in some sort of trouble, and he needed Carly’s help, whether he could it admit or not.

How could she help him if she didn’t even know what was wrong?

“You won’t do that,” Lyle said grimly.

“I will.”

“Just don’t. Put it back, OK? Forget all about it.”

Carly’s own hands were shaking now as she struggled clumsily with the bag’s zipper. Lyle reached out again to snatch it from her, but she turned away from him and managed to get the zipper open.

Her eyes fell on all the ordinary items—a few clothes and a plastic bag holding an electric razor, a bottle of aftershave, toothpaste, a toothbrush, and … something else …

Carly reached for the amber-colored plastic vial half-full of white tablets. She picked it up and looked at it. There was no label.

This is it, she realized.

This is what Lyle didn't want me to find.

CHAPTER TWENTY SEVEN

Carly waved the tinted plastic vial in front of Lyle's face.

"What is this?" she demanded.

"Put it back."

"Tell me."

"It's none of your business."

"It sure as hell is my business. I'm your partner, Lyle. This kind of thing affects us both as a team. I need to know."

Lyle put his hand against the car and leaned as if he needed it for support.

"Let's at least get back in the car, OK?" he said.

It took Carly a moment to register what he meant. The two of them were standing out in the open in a parking lot outside Harmonium's City Hall. Their argument was getting loud, and she was clutching his go-bag while waving a suspicious bottle in his face.

The situation was already bad enough without making a public spectacle of it.

Still holding the vial, Carly dropped Lyle's bag back into the trunk and slammed the lid shut. They each turned and walked their separate ways back to the car doors. She got into the passenger seat, and Lyle slid back behind the wheel. They closed the car doors and sat there for a moment, not looking at each other.

Then, gripping the vial tightly, Carly held it out between them.

"What are these pills, Lyle? And don't tell me it's some sort of prescription. There's no label. Besides, you wouldn't have panicked like that if it was anything you were supposed to have."

"It's a sedative," Lyle murmured.

"What kind of sedative?"

"Lorazepam."

Carly was sure she'd heard the word before, but she really knew nothing about it. This wasn't an ordinary street drug.

"Where did you get it?"

"From … a contact."

"So it's a controlled substance?"

"Right. But widely used medically."

"Does it have side effects?"

"Tiredness mostly."

"But it has a high potential for abuse?"

"It's an anti-anxiety medication, among other things."

That hadn't answered her question, but she was sure potential abuse was an issue. And she also suspected he was being deliberately vague about the side effects.

Of course she and Lyle both had unsavory criminal contacts who could supply them with all kinds of controlled substances. Carly wasn't interested in finding out just who Lyle's supplier was, at least not right now. She had much more serious problems to deal with.

Her heart sank as she remembered what Lyle had said earlier today.

"Carly, I haven't been drinking."

He hadn't been lying to her—not exactly. But he hadn't been honest either. He'd been selectively truthful and deliberately evasive.

The way addicts are.

It was a shocking realization. Lyle had never made a secret of his past struggles with alcohol. He'd been open and upfront with her about all that. He'd been proud of staying sober. This was the first time he'd ever deceived her in a manner typical of an addict.

"You shouldn't have gone through my things, Carly," he muttered bitterly.

"Maybe not. But what would have happened if I hadn't? I need to know this kind of thing Lyle."

She opened the vial and dropped a single pill into her palm. It had an indented line across the center.

"How much do you take?" she asked.

"You're supposed to break the pill in half."

"Supposed to?"

Lyle hit the steering wheel with his fists.

"Damn it, Carly, what do you expect me to tell you? Whatever I say, you'll think I'm lying."

He's probably right, she thought.

She saw that her partner looked broken and exhausted and on the verge of tears.

She reached over and touched him on the shoulder.

"Lyle, something triggered this," she said. "It was our last case, wasn't it? It was getting injected with that paralytic drug. I can imagine how awful that must have been for you—"

"No, I don't think you can," Lyle interrupted. "Carly it scared the living hell out of me …"

His voice faded, and his chest heaved in a single sob.

"I'm scared to death … of losing you. I mean of seeing you die in some awful situation like that. Of being helpless to stop it."

Carly felt a surge of comprehension.

Her own life had been in danger when Lyle was helpless. He hadn't been able to do a single thing to save her. And that must have seemed too much like the way he lost his previous partner.

Of course. Lyle wasn't able to save Dawn.

And now she remembered what Dawn's spirit had said in her recent dream vision.

"Carly, he's going to hurt himself unless you stop him."

This must be exactly what that warning had meant. Even from beyond death, Lyle's previous partner had seen this danger for him. She had done her best to warn Carly about it.

Carly's throat was tight with emotion.

I should have listened to her better.

I should have done something already.

For a moment she felt tempted to tell him about her communication with Dawn, and how she'd said she always watched over Lyle, and how worried she was about him.

No, don't, she warned herself.

It had been just a little while since she'd even begun to admit her contacts with the dead. He hadn't taken it well, and for good reason. She knew very well that it was an extraordinary issue and impossible for most people to deal with at all.

She'd been keeping the truth from him for much too long, but this wasn't the time to push him any further. Lyle was much too fragile right now to hear that Dawn was talking to her from beyond the grave. It might even put him over some kind of desperate edge. Carly couldn't take a chance on that.

Besides, there was a much more basic issue to deal with.

She spoke slowly and cautiously.

"Lyle, I'm sure you understand … we can't keep on working this way."

"What do you mean?"

"I mean working together, on this case, right now. Surely you can see that you came back to work too quickly. You need to …"

Carly paused for a moment, then added, "Well, I don't know exactly what you need to do, but it sure isn't being out here on this case."

"So what are you saying? That we should give up and go back to Quantico?"

"No, that's not what I'm saying."

"Then what? Carly, there's still a serial killer out there. More people are going to die. And I can't just leave you here to work this case on your own."

"You don't have to, Lyle. Voss can send somebody else out to take over for you. Not everybody was out on assignment when we left. George Allen is a good agent, and I'm sure he's available. If we get in touch with Voss right now, Agent Allen can be here in just a few hours."

"But what are we … ?"

Lyle's voice faltered, but Carly knew what he wanted to ask.

What are we going to tell Voss?

She'd promised Voss to let him know if Lyle started drinking, and of course he'd want her to tell him about the sedatives as well. But now that she was faced with the reality of that option, she wondered …

Can I really do that?

It would be an irrevocable step with enormous consequences.

She knew that the time might eventually come for that. But surely that time hadn't yet arrived.

"You can just tell Voss the truth—or the part of the truth that really matters right now. Tell him you realized he was right from the start to worry about putting you on a case. Tell him you really weren't ready. He'll understand. He's your friend, Lyle. He cares about you. We'll work out the rest of it later."

Lyle didn't say anything. He looked like he was being crushed under some massive weight.

"This is the right thing to do," Carly said.

Lyle nodded miserably.

"I just hate this, Carly. I've been a good agent for a long time."

"The best," Carly said, taking his hand. "I hate it too. But this isn't your fault. I know you feel awfully weak right now, but you're not weak. You're the strongest person I know—the strongest person I've ever known. You can get through this. And you don't have to do it alone."

She squeezed his hand tightly.

"I'm on your side, Lyle," she said. "I'm your friend. I care about you. I'm here for you. I'll help you in any way I can."

Lyle squeezed her hand back.

"I know," he said in a thick, soft voice. "Thanks."

They both fell silent for a moment. Carly welcomed the quiet after all the chaos they'd been through today. And Lyle's face had stopped twitching and his teeth had stopped grinding. He looked positively calm.

Maybe he's healing already.

Finally Lyle took a long, slow breath.

"Okay let's do this. Let's go back to the hotel. I'll get myself together there and call Voss. And I'll book a flight to Quantico and book a shuttle to take me to the Pittsburgh International Airport. Meanwhile …"

He paused for a moment, then took the keys out of the ignition and handed them to Carly.

"Maybe you should drive," he said.

"I suppose so," Carly said.

They both got out of the car and switched places. Carly started the engine and drove them down the steep hillside with its narrow streets and small houses, then past the boarded-up businesses in the downtown area. She realized again what a depressing city Harmonium was.

Hardly the place for Lyle right now.

When they parked in front of the rundown Cameron Hotel, Lyle managed a weak smile.

"Thanks, Carly," he said before he got out of the car.

"No thanks are necessary," Carly said with a smile. "We're still partners."

"What are you going to do until Agent Allen or somebody else gets here to replace me?"

"I'll keep working the case."

"But Carly—"

"I won't do anything dangerous, I promise."

Lyle looked at her skeptically.

"I've heard that before," he said. "Maybe I could just hang around until my replacement gets here."

Carly felt an almost irresistible urge to say yes to this idea. But she quickly realized what would happen if she and Lyle kept working together even for a few more minutes. Pretty soon they'd be caught up in their brainstorming and pretending to themselves and each other that nothing was wrong with Lyle. It would be a huge setback for him.

Best to make a clean break—at least for now.

"You go," she said. "Get yourself better."

"But—"

"I really mean it, Lyle. I'll be all right. I'm sure we won't be making any arrests until Agent Allen gets here. But if we do, I'll make sure Chief Tallarico has got my back. Meanwhile I can keep looking for leads. I'll stay out of trouble."

"You'd better," Lyle said with a stern wag of his finger.

"It'll be boring, I promise," Carly said with a chuckle.

With a brief laugh, Lyle got out of the car. He retrieved his go-bag, which no longer had the pills in it, out of the trunk and then trudged away into the hotel entrance.

Carly felt her eyes fill up with tears. She hated to leave him like this, but she knew she didn't have any real choice.

She quickly dried her eyes. Before she turned the ignition, she took out the vial and looked at it. She'd been on edge herself during the last couple of days, and she could understand the temptation to do just about anything to settle one's nerves.

It's so easy to slip, she thought.

Not just for Lyle, but for anyone.

Meanwhile, she needed some coffee and something to eat in order to get her thoughts together. As she drove toward the fast food place where she and Lyle had eaten breakfast that morning, her own words echoed through her mind.

"I won't do anything dangerous, I promise."

She'd meant it when she'd said it to Lyle, and she hoped it was a promise she could keep.

But what if danger comes looking for me?

CHAPTER TWENTY EIGHT

I shouldn't let her see me, the man thought.

As he rounded the end of the supermarket aisle, the woman had come into view near the refrigerated goods. She was an elderly woman wearing a jogging suit, and she appeared to be in fine shape for someone her age. With that healthy complexion and sleek, full, snowy-white hair, no one would guess what she must be going through right now.

He ducked his head under his fedora and stared at the nearest shelf, pretending to be making a choice of cleaning products. Not that it would be a disaster if she did see him and even recognize him. She'd have no cause for surprise to run into him here. He'd have no trouble engaging in conversation with her for a few moments.

But he preferred to stay out of sight. His observations were so important at this point in the process.

He reminded himself of her name.

Maureen Johnson ...

... and her husband's name was Timothy.

He knew that just a couple of days ago Maureen Johnson had experienced the most terrible tragedy of her life.

Today he'd been following her ever since she'd left her house a while ago, keeping a car or two behind as she drove to this supermarket. He'd parked in the nearby lot and watched her go inside the store, then waited quietly in his car until she'd been in the store for a few minutes.

Then he'd come inside and chosen a cart and wandered the aisles looking for her, picking up random items and putting them into his cart in order to look like an ordinary shopper. He figured he'd just abandon the cart when he was ready to go and leave without buying anything.

And now, here she was, looking healthy and anything but distraught.

For a moment, the man felt a spasm of doubt.

Maybe I was wrong.

Maybe she wasn't as devastated as she'd seemed the day before yesterday, when he'd stood beside her as she looked down at her husband's dead body. She'd actually fallen to her knees and let out a keening wail.

"How could you do this to me, Timothy?" she'd sobbed. *"Now I've got no one left, and nothing to live for. Why couldn't you have taken me with you?"*

He'd offered her a handkerchief and some words of comfort. But at the time, she'd been so helpless with grief that she'd seemed barely aware of his attentions.

Now here she was, shopping for groceries, looking as if nothing in her life could possibly be wrong.

Except for one thing …

He smiled when it came to his attention.

I should have noticed right away.

Her shopping cart was empty. By now she should have picked up at least a few items. Instead, she was standing in front of the refrigerated goods staring at a row of milk cartons.

But not really looking at them at all.

Her eyes weren't focused on anything. She'd slipped into a mini-trance right where she was standing. She had probably forgotten where she was or why she'd come here.

That's grief, he thought.

That's inconsolable grief.

He'd seen enough of it to know it when he saw it. What's more, she reminded him of somebody from his childhood.

Who was that woman?

He tried to recall as he added another random item to his cart and shuffled a little ways along the aisle. There had been so many …

Then he remembered, although he still had no idea what her name had been. She'd just been another dead body in storage in his father's funeral home. It had been one of those nights when his father had flown into one of his rages—he couldn't remember now what his fault had been, and he probably hadn't even known at the time. Father's rages had seemed almost random, and as a boy he'd always been helpless against that fury.

As he often did, Father had locked him up in the storage room with the cadavers.

As usual, Father had first removed all the lightbulbs from their sockets.

The boy had been left in total darkness for whole nights at a time with no one to keep him company.

No one but dead people.

The man smiled at the memory as the woman stepped away from the milk cartons and walked over to peer vacantly at the cheeses.

Poor Father, he thought.

He'd had no idea what effect his "punishments" really had on his son.

Oh, the first few times he'd been locked up like that—when he was five or six years old, maybe—he'd been terrified out of his mind and had shrieked all night to high heaven, but to no avail. There had been no sympathetic ear within earshot, no one to save him.

But after a couple of years, something had changed. He'd learned to grope his way around the pitch-dark storage room as well as if he'd been able to see. And he'd started opening up the refrigerator units and pulling out the rolling racks where the corpses were kept.

Although he couldn't see them, he'd finger the naked cadavers from head to foot, and after a time they didn't even seem cold anymore, and the formaldehyde smell seemed as sweet as lilacs. The bodies never moved, and they certainly never spoke, but he knew they were there for him, and they cared about him.

They were his trusted companions. He'd spend whole nights at a time talking to them, often crying as they listened to him spill out his soul to them, all the pains and heartaches and humiliations he experienced during every single day of his childhood. And sometimes he'd laugh wildly and uncontrollably with sheer relief to know that someone didn't hate him, that somebody understood.

The man sighed at the beautiful memory.

And yes, the woman reminded him of one of those corpses. He'd never known the dead woman's name, and he'd never even seen her—not with his eyes, anyway. But in the dark he'd learned her face by heart through the tips of his fingers.

And now here was that face again, standing just a short distance away from him.

He smiled. It somehow seemed more than a mere coincidence that he was now seeing a face with his eyes that he had once "seen" through his fingers.

It must mean something, he thought.

Perhaps it was a reminder of the sheer goodness of his mission in life—to send unhappy souls to eternal bliss, over and over again until all the pain in the world was at an end …

And may I be the last to join them.

The woman was still staring at the cheeses, truly lost in her mute, all-numbing trance. Then she turned away from the refrigeration unit and said a single word.

The man couldn't hear the word, but he knew what it was.

It was her husband's name.

"Timothy."

She'd turned toward her husband reflexively, expecting to ask his advice on which item to buy. Instead, she let out a gasp to see there was nobody there.

The poor woman, the man thought.

She could go on for years like this, discovering this perpetual absence over and over again, stabbed to the heart every single time by the dull, cruel, cold blade of grief, unless …

Unless I end it for her with my own sharper and kinder and much swifter blade.

She'd never be able to thank him, at least not in words, but he'd feel her palpable and eternal gratitude as her life slipped out of her body. And he'd feel that again whenever he thought about her in the future.

Now the woman was looking into her grocery cart, seeming to notice that it was still empty. The man recognized another sort of realization in her eyes.

She knows it's pointless.

Coming here and shopping.

Food and sustenance and anything life-giving.

There's no use in any of it.

Sure enough, she turned and walked away from her shopping cart and headed out of the store. In her faltering gait the man could see her despair, and he felt it in the very depths of his own soul.

He knew exactly what that poor woman needed.

And I'll be there to grant her wish.

He reached into his pocket and fingered the new penny inside.

CHAPTER TWENTY NINE

Carly didn't much like what she was seeing.

From where she was sitting at a plastic table in the fast food restaurant, nibbling on a hamburger and sipping coffee, she really couldn't avoid viewing what was on the big TV screen.

I hope Lyle isn't watching this too, she thought.

Her partner was already discouraged enough without finding out about the local news. There on the screen was Mayor Freelander, standing in front of City Hall and holding forth to a group of reporters. The sound was off, but closed captions appearing below him gave Carly a pretty good glimpse of what the mayor was talking about. And it wasn't going to be helpful to this case at all.

With the aid of the FBI, the mayor announced, the local police had arrested a suspect in the three recent murders.

And yes, Freelander added, the evidence against this suspect was all but conclusive.

But no, he wasn't ready to reveal the suspect's name.

Carly gave a deep sigh.

Tallarico sure was right.

She remembered the note of resignation in the chief's voice when he was on his way to the mayor's office.

"I'd better go and try to talk sense to him," he'd said. *"Not much chance of success though."*

Carly was livid. She wondered, did the mayor have the slightest inkling the trouble he was causing, not just to the investigation but possibly the city he cared so much about?

At least she could see that Tallarico wasn't stranded at the mayor's side, like he'd been during the media gathering this morning. He wasn't going to have to parrot whatever foolishness the mayor was spouting.

Then a reporter interrupted Mayor Freelander with a loud question, "Is it true the suspect is a cop?"

For a moment the mayor looked flustered. The reporter had obviously sniffed out something about the arrest in the police station.

He has to be wondering just how much more that guy knows.

Freelander quickly repeated that he wasn't ready to reveal anything about the suspect's identity. Then he cut off the questions and went back to making comments of his own, praising the police and staff and even the FBI agents, all of whom, he said, had worked so well under his direction.

Just as the mayor was finishing his comments, Carly's phone buzzed.

Her heart jumped when she saw that the call was from Special Agent Preston Voss in Quantico.

I should have expected this, she thought, accepting the call.

"Agent See, I got a phone call from Agent Ramsey a little while ago," Voss said. "He requested that I send a replacement for him to Harmonium to work with you on the serial case. He specifically asked for Special Agent George Allen. I'm calling to let you know Allen's on his way there right now. I assume that's all right with you."

"That's fine, thanks," Carly said, gulping down a knot of worry. "Agent Ramsey and I discussed everything, including his replacement."

Am I going to have to explain it all right now? she wondered.

She could hear concern in the team chief's voice, but she didn't know exactly what Lyle had told him.

Meanwhile, she heard a beep that announced someone else was trying to call her at this very moment.

Is it Lyle?

Even if it was, she couldn't interrupt her call with Voss to answer.

I'll get back to him as soon as I'm finished.

"Agent Allen should be there in just a few hours," Voss continued. "Meanwhile, I want you to be careful. Don't go trying anything on your own without your partner there. Do you hear me?"

"I hear you."

"I mean it, Agent See. You've got a bit of a reputation for getting yourself into trouble."

"I understand, sir. I'll be careful, sir."

"OK, then."

A long silence fell. Carly found it hard to breathe.

Is he expecting me to say something more?

She and Lyle had agreed on what he should say to the team chief.

"Tell him you really weren't ready. He'll understand."

At the time, it had seemed like the best approach would be not telling Chief Voss absolutely everything about Lyle's state of mind. At least not right now. For everyone's sake, they really just needed to make Lyle's removal and replacement as straightforward and painless as possible.

But of course, conversations didn't always go as planned. Had Lyle told Voss enough? Or had he told him too little? Right now Carly wished they'd made the call together so she'd have a better idea of what had transpired.

And how much did Voss expect to hear from her right now?

Meanwhile, the insistent beeping had stopped. Whoever was trying to call her had given up, at least for the moment.

Carly suddenly thought of something Voss needed to know.

"Sir, you might be getting word through the media that we've already solved the case. The mayor made that announcement just now to a bunch of reporters. Obviously, he doesn't know what he's talking about."

Chief Voss heaved an anxious-sounding sigh.

"Thanks for letting me know," he said. "We'll talk again when you're finished with this case. That's all for now."

Carly exhaled with relief as the chief ended the call. The inevitable discussion about Lyle had been postponed, at least. She still didn't know how much Voss knew or what he was going to do, but she remembered what she had told Lyle.

"He's your friend, Lyle. He cares about you."

She thought it was likely that Voss would do whatever he could to deal with Lyle's problem in as painless a manner as possible.

Then Carly remembered the beeping she'd heard during that call.

Was it Lyle?

If it was, she'd better get back to him right away.

She picked up her phone and checked her incoming calls. But her heart sank to see that the call hadn't been from Lyle.

It was from her own mother.

Not now, Mom.

Her conversations with her mother tended to be fraught and stressful, and Carly felt too stressed already. And yet, if she let the call go unanswered, she knew it would nag at her for the rest of the day, distracting her from her work on the case. Besides, her mother was likely to call back at some inopportune time.

Reluctantly, she returned the call.

"Hi, Carly, dear," her mother said when she answered.

"Hi, Mom."

Then her mother spoke haltingly.

"I was wondering … if there was any news … I mean, have you

found out anything about …"

Mom's voice faded, and for a moment Carly wondered whether she was asking about the case at hand. But of course Mom had no way of knowing about the case or even where Carly was right now.

Carly stifled a groan of dismay as she realized what Mom meant.

She sure got to the point fast.

Mom wanted to know whether Carly had learned anything about her sister, Megan.

Last month, during a visit home in Currie, Illinois, Carly had finally told Mom about her mysterious ability. And Mom had told Carly something she hadn't known before—that Carly's grandmother had possessed a similar gift.

Carly had also told Mom she'd received a message suggesting that Megan was alive. She'd quickly wondered whether this had been a mistake. Mom had become quite agitated about the possibility, and she'd vented her frustration at Carly.

"If your sister is alive, it's up to you to find her," she'd said emphatically.

Carly had tried to explain that she had tried everything she could think of already, including non-mystical resources at her disposal as an FBI agent. But Mom had reacted badly—or at least very emotionally.

"I don't even know why you bothered to come home if this is all you've got to say," she'd said. *"I just don't understand."*

And now, what was Carly going to say? Should she tell her mother all about that trip to California and her fruitless visit to the island wildlife refuge of Santa Novara? She didn't see how she could do that without confusing Mom and upsetting her all over again. Anyhow, Carly hadn't found out anything helpful on that venture.

"Mom, I've been doing everything I can. And I'll keep doing everything I can."

"But do you still think Megan is alive?"

"I don't know Mom, I … I guess I don't have any reason to think otherwise."

Except, she thought with a shiver, for the name Native Americans had given to those islands in the past.

Islands of the Dead.

But it surely wasn't a good idea to mention that to Mom at the moment.

"Are you looking for her right now?" Mom asked.

"No, Mom I'm working on a murder case."

"Well, can't you set the case aside for a while and—?"

"Mom, I *can't* stop working on this case," Carly gently interrupted. "I'm hunting down a serial killer in Harmonium, Pennsylvania. If I don't stop him, he'll kill again. It's likely that he's chosen his next victim already."

Mom let out a gasp of excitement.

"Oh, then maybe I can help!" she said. "I mean, the sooner you solve this case, the sooner you can get back to looking for your sister."

Carly held back a sigh.

"It's nice of you to offer, Mom, but …"

Carly's voice faded for a moment as she realized something. Mom *had* been a real help a couple of cases ago when she and Lyle had hunted down a killer obsessed with Shakespeare. As a community college professor and a frustrated scholar, Mom had all kinds of information in her head, especially about literature, legend, and folklore. Maybe, just maybe, Mom might have insights to offer about this mystery.

There were several puzzling aspects to this case that she hadn't had time to research.

Maybe Mom can help.

CHAPTER THIRTY

"Mom, what can you tell me about St. Genesius?" Carly said.

"Why do you ask?"

"One of the victims was wearing a St. Genesius medallion."

"Oh, then the victim must have been involved with theater somehow. Some theater people wear a medallion like that. It usually has an inscription that says, 'St. Genesius, pray for us.'"

Carly felt a hopeful tingle.

"Yes, this medallion had that inscription," she said. "The victim's widow said he'd once wanted to be an actor. Who was St. Genesius, anyway?"

"The patron saint of actors," Mom said. "According to the story, Genesius was a Roman actor during the third century, in the time of Emperor Diocletian. Genesius was a believer in the Roman gods, and he liked to make fun of the new religion of Christianity. And then one day … let's see if I remember this right."

Mom paused for a moment.

"He was performing a play for the emperor—a satire about Christianity. In it he pretended to be baptized. It was supposed to be funny—a joke. But during his mock-baptism, the whole thing turned real, and Genesius became a Christian believer. Nobody could talk him out of his newfound faith, not even the emperor, so he wound up being martyred—beheaded, I believe. That's about all I know about him. Do you want me to find out some more?"

Carly thought for a moment. The story was certainly interesting, and it was easy to see how St. Genesius had become the patron saint of actors. But did it have anything to do with the case at hand?

Probably not, she realized.

The medallion had been stolen by Officer Ross Campbell, who now seemed to be an unlikely suspect for the murders. The real killer had apparently left the medallion alone, which suggested that he didn't care about St. Genesius or his story.

But there was something else that had been troubling her.

"Is there something significant about a penny?" she asked.

"Be more specific, dear. Do you mean the coin? Or the girl's name?"

"The coin."

"Well, nobody uses them anymore. I've read that they cost more to make than they're worth. I thought they were going to stop making them."

"Do they stand for something?"

"Penny-pinching, I suppose. Miserliness. Cheapskate."

Penny-pinching? Carly thought.

"Mom, I'm going to tell you something we don't want the public to know. I hope it goes without saying that you can't tell anybody else at all about it."

"Of course."

"We found a penny with each murder victim. But cheapskate doesn't seem to fit, at least not with anything we've learned so far. I mean, I don't think the killer is some kind of miser. One victim was a homeless man. The other two were women with pretty ordinary lifestyles."

"Ah. Well, I can think of some possibilities. Were the coins placed on the eyelids? Or the tongue?"

"No, the killer seems to have put the pennies in their hands either before or after he killed them. Can you think of what that means?"

"Well, if they were on the eyelids I'd say it was probably an ancient Celtic thing. And a penny in the mouth could be from Greek and Latin mythology to pay for passage to the land of the dead. But I suppose it's the penny itself that matters, not where it wound up."

Carly waited impatiently during another silence. This time she heard Mom thumbing through pages in a book.

"Yes, it really does sound to me like a Greek or Latin thing," Mom finally said. "Like someone was preparing the dead person to pay Charon."

The name vaguely rang a bell for Carly, but she couldn't quite place it.

"Please explain," she said.

"Well, in Greek mythology, Charon was the ferryman to the Underworld."

Carly's pulse quickened at the word "ferryman." She flashed back to those visions in which she'd found herself on a modern-day ferryboat loaded with coffins instead of cars.

"Please tell me more."

"Well, Charon's job was to transport the souls of the recently dead across the River Styx to the Underworld, where the god Hades ruled over the dead. But the dead had to be properly prepared for the journey, with proper funeral rites. And when somebody died in Ancient Greece … oh, I do hope this is helpful, Carly."

"Keep going," Carly said breathlessly.

"The recently departed's friends and loved ones would put a coin on his or her tongue to pay for the ferry trip. Without it, those departed souls couldn't afford Charon's fare. They might wind up wandering the shore along the River Styx for hundreds of years until Charon decided to ferry them over anyway."

Carly's brain was clicking away excitedly, trying to process what she was hearing. Meanwhile, she could hear Mom turning more pages.

"There's a description of Charon in Virgil's epic poem, the *Aeneid,"* Mom said. "Oh, yes, here it is. He seems to have been an ugly sort of fellow …"

Mom read aloud:

… A sordid god: down from his hairy chin
A length of beard descends, uncombed, unclean;
His eyes, like hollow furnaces on fire;
A girdle, foul with grease, binds his obscene attire.

"Do you suppose this awful killer is a scholar of some kind?" Mom asked. "I don't think it would be the first time that a scholar turned to murder."

Carly thought for a moment. Certainly Campbell didn't qualify as a scholar. Might the Rev. Miles Lindsay be up on rituals for the dead in other cultures? Carly quickly reminded herself that Lindsay now seemed like an unlikely suspect. For that matter, so did Campbell.

"Perhaps he imagines he's Charon himself," Mom added.

"I don't know, Mom. But I think this might be really helpful information. Thanks. I've got to go now."

"OK. Just solve this case quickly so you can get back to looking for your sister."

Carly shook her head.

"Mom, I don't think you should …"

"I know, I shouldn't get my hopes up. Well, I'll try my best. But you try your best too. Now go ahead and get back to work."

The call ended, and Carly stared into space for a few moments. The image of a ferryboat loaded with coffins was starting to make sense now.

"Charon," she murmured aloud.

She wondered—was Mom right in suggesting the killer actually imagined himself to be the mythical ferryman Charon?

No, it doesn't seem quite right, she thought.

After all, Charon was supposed to *receive* the coin, not actually give it to his passengers. Instead, Carly guessed, if the murders were connected to that legend, the killer must be preparing his victims for safe passage to the hereafter. Maybe the coins were meant as a sort of final blessing.

A few pieces seemed to be coming together in Carly's mind now. As Lyle had said, the killer was no sadist.

Maybe he really does see himself as an angel of mercy.

If so, all he wanted to do was free his victims from their grief and heartache through the eternal comfort of death.

The thought made her shudder. Could some misplaced sense of kindness really be a motive for murder? In some ways, that was a more horrifying notion than the usual motives of hatred or revenge.

Even so, Carly couldn't deny the feeling that she was finally on the right track. But did she really have any better idea than before who actually might be the killer?

Maybe so, she realized.

Maybe, she thought, the killer was somebody who felt a close kinship with the dead. Maybe he was someone who worked in a funeral home—an undertaker, perhaps, or some sort of assistant.

This gave her something tangible to talk over with Chief Tallarico. Maybe he knew a few dark secrets about Harmonium's bustling death business—including funeral directors with less than savory pasts. Or maybe someone with a more scholarly past than they'd yet considered.

She finished the last bites of her burger and swallowed the rest of her coffee, then headed outside. Dusk was falling, and the downtown streets were nearly deserted.

Then, just as she approached her vehicle, she heard a soft voice speak from somewhere very close to her.

"Look!"

CHAPTER THIRTY ONE

Carly looked all around, but she saw no one nearby. And yet she was sure she'd heard someone speak.

And now the voice came again.

"Just look ..."

At first, Carly thought it was an ordinary voice, like an ordinary person speaking urgently. But no one was close enough to have given her that order.

No living person, she realized.

Was this a message from the dead?

But she wasn't in the presence of a corpse. She wasn't even in contact with anything belonging to a victim in this case. She wondered if she was hallucinating. Was the stress of dealing with her partner's personal torments interfering with her instincts?

But then the voice came again.

"Young lady ... look ... just turn and look ..."

Carly turned around

The only thing nearby was a newspaper vending box. As she stood there staring at it, she heard the murmuring voice again.

"Just look."

The sound seemed to be coming from that box. That certainly seemed crazy, but Carly had dealt with a lot of crazy things in her strange life.

As she took a step toward the newspaper box, the voice repeated its plaintive phrase.

"Just look."

Her doubts were dispelled. The voice was real. It was a man's voice, and of course it had to be the voice of some departed spirit.

But why would it be reaching out to her from a newspaper box?

She crouched in front of the box and muttered under her breath.

"Look at what?"

"Just look," the voice repeated.

Carly stifled a groan of irritation. Why did the voices of the dead have to be like this sometimes? It was bad enough that they could be vague and riddling. Sometimes they didn't even seem to have any idea of what they wanted to say. And how could this voice even be connected with her investigation at all?

"I don't understand," she said.

"Just look."

There was nothing to see except the front page of today's local newspaper displayed behind the glass front of the box. The headline had to do with the mayor's plans to revitalize Harmonium. Was the voice trying to alert her to that news story? She couldn't imagine why.

"Just look," the voice said again.

"Look where?"

"Look closer."

There was only one way to "look closer." She inserted a couple of dollar bills into the vending slot and bought a newspaper. Skimming the front page, she saw nothing that might be pertinent.

She heard the voice again, and now it seemed to come from within the newspaper itself.

"Look."

"But where?"

No reply came, but suddenly the answer seemed obvious to Carly.

The obituaries,

Leaning against the vending box, Carly thumbed through the small local newspaper until she came to the obituary page. It was full of names and mostly short, perfunctory items about those people. The items seemed less like obituaries than like classified ads.

She remembered what Lyle had said about Harmonium.

"Death seems to be the only growing industry around here."

But one obituary was more detailed than the others. Its headline was at the top of the page, and it had a photograph of its subject. The headline read:

Beloved Retired Schoolteacher Dies in Car Accident

The photograph was of a smiling, elderly man. His name, according to the obituary, was Timothy Johnson, and he'd died after losing control of his vehicle on a rainy day and driving off a cliff.

"Is this you?" Carly whispered to the picture

When there was no reply, she asked, "Was this no accident? Were you a victim?"

"Just look," the voice said yet again.

Carly rolled her eyes with frustration.

Can't he say anything else at all? Is this just a waste of time?

She was in the middle of an important investigation. What could an auto accident have to do with a series of knife murders?

Even so, the voice intrigued her. It sounded like it was speaking with great effort. Maybe it just couldn't tell her more.

She put her mind to work on this riddling communication.

A well-loved man had died unexpectedly.

That surely meant that there would be a mourners.

And the serial killer that she was chasing had killed people who were mourning a recent death.

That must be the connection.

This departed spirit could be trying to warn her that one of his loved ones was in danger.

Did this mean she could stop another murder from happening?

But she saw from the newspaper story that it wasn't going to be that easy. Timothy Johnson had left behind a fair number of survivors—his wife Maureen, his elder sister Lynn, three sons and two daughters, eight grandchildren, and two great-grandchildren. Most of these survivors lived in Harmonium.

She murmured to the picture, "Is one of these people in danger?"

There was a silence. And then the voice replied weakly.

"Yes."

Carly felt a tingle of excitement run through her whole body. This was her chance to stop another death. Maybe even to trap the murderer in his attempt to kill again.

"Who is it? " she whispered.

"I can't ..." the voice replied.

"Can't tell me? Why not?"

For a moment all she heard was a weak moan. Then the voice whispered faintly.

"*Come closer.*"

"I don't understand."

"*You need to be ...*"

The voice trailed off and Carly received no further reply. The message had come to an abrupt and inconclusive end.

What could "come closer" mean? How did she "need to be"?

She placed her hand on the photograph of Timothy Johnson but felt no connection.

The spirit was gone.

Leaning more heavily on the vending box, Carly lowered the

newspaper to her side. She wondered—what could she possibly do with this communication?

Does it mean anything at all?

She couldn't even be sure it was Timothy Johnson's spirit she'd just heard from. After all, there were lots of other names on that obituary page. Johnson's just happened to be the most prominent, with a headline and photograph above the fold.

And if it *had* been Johnson's spirit, which one of his listed family members most shared that essential trait that the killer seemed to seek out in his victims—profound and inconsolable grief for a departed loved one? There were some half-dozen possible targets listed in the obituary.

Should she just start trying to contact them?

And tell them what?

Carly took a few deep, slow breaths, trying to clear her head. She replayed in her mind the last words the spirit had said to her.

"Come closer."

Again she wondered—come where?

The answer suddenly seemed clear. After all, her strongest communications with the dead tended to be when she was in close proximity to their bodies—ideally actually touching those bodies. The obituary had said that Timothy Johnson had died the day before yesterday.

If so, there was one obvious place where Carly should go look for him.

The city morgue!

The body was probably still in storage there. But how was she going to get a look at it—or better yet, to actually touch it?

Yesterday Chief Tallarico had given Carly and Lyle a list of pertinent contact information, including phone numbers for people and departments involved with the case. Carly took out her phone and punched in the cellphone number for the coroner, Dr. Simon Russo.

He answered quickly, and Carly told him who was calling.

"This is a bit of a surprise, Agent See," the coroner said in a cheerful voice. "How may I help you?"

Carly felt momentarily stymied.

How am I going to explain this? she thought.

It would be best if she didn't try to explain it at all—if she could persuade Russo to just let her look at the body without going into any details. But it was going to be hard to pull off a gambit like that on the phone.

I'd better talk to him in person.

"I know it's after hours," Carly said, "and you've probably left work for the day, but I wondered if maybe the two of us could meet at the morgue shortly."

The coroner chuckled pleasantly.

"As it happens, I'm still here, hard at work. So by all means, drop on by. The building's locked, but if you ring when you get here, I can let you in."

"Thanks," Carly said. "That would be a great help."

Carly ended the call. She felt slightly giddy as she headed toward her parked car. But she scolded herself not to get her hopes up. For all she knew, this errand wasn't going to end any better than yesterday's trip to the cemetery.

Something good will come of this, she thought as she turned on the ignition and started driving toward City Hall.

It just has to.

CHAPTER THIRTY TWO

Lyle stood looking out his hotel window into the deepening twilight. It was somehow eerie to see the usual lights on tall poles glowing over those nearly empty streets. There were almost no pedestrians or traffic to be seen—as if the dying town of Harmonium was determined to keep going without any living people in it at all.

Turning away from the window, he stepped over to the bed and stretched out on it with his shoes on. He was grateful for one thing—that Carly had taken his pills away. If they were within reach right now, he wouldn't be able to resist their pull.

Just a few minutes ago Lyle had gone online to book a shuttle to Pittsburgh International Airport and a commercial flight to Reagan International Airport. But the shuttle wasn't going to arrive for a while, and the flight wasn't for another four hours.

Meanwhile, he had to pass the time somehow, and his mind kept returning to the case.

Not your assignment anymore, he told himself. *Let it go.*

But it wasn't easy to suddenly shift his brain to neutral after all the mental effort he'd been putting in with his partner to find the serial killer.

She's not your partner at the moment, he reminded himself.

And yet—that wasn't really true. Carly had said so herself. She'd also said they were much more than partners.

"I'm your friend. I care about you. I'm here for you. I'll help you in any way I can."

It's got to be a two-way street, he thought.

If there was even the slightest chance he could be of help to Carly, he couldn't let it pass by. He reached for his cellphone and punched in her number, then heard Carly's voice answer.

"Hey," he said. "I hope I'm not bothering you."

"No," she replied, not exactly convincingly.

He didn't hear any irritation in her voice, but she did sound preoccupied.

Not surprising. She's still on the job.

"Maybe I should leave you alone," Lyle said. "It sounds like maybe you're in the middle of something. A lead, maybe?"

"Could be. It's hard to say just yet. Are you on your way to the airport?"

"No, the shuttle isn't going to get here for a little while."

An awkward silence fell. Lyle knew that he ought to end the call, but he wasn't ready to do that yet. He recognized some familiar car sounds and realized that she must be driving.

"Are you going somewhere?" he asked.

"Yeah, to the city morgue."

"Isn't it closed for the day?"

"It is. But Dr. Russo said he'd meet me there."

"What kind of lead have you got?"

He heard Carly let out a sad sigh.

"Oh, Lyle, let's not get into all this. We've made a decision, OK? It was the right decision. If you and I start talking about this case, before we know it we'll change our minds and forget everything that's wrong, and you'll be back working with me, and …"

Her voice fell silent.

"You're right," Lyle told her. "I'm sorry I called."

"Don't be sorry."

Another silence fell.

Just get off the phone, Lyle tried to tell himself.

But still he hesitated.

"Lyle, I won't lie to you," Carly's words tumbled out in a rush. "I don't like working without you. And working with Agent Allen isn't going to be the same. Actually, it's going to feel weird. I miss you already."

Not as much as I miss you, Lyle thought.

But it seemed best not to say those words aloud.

"Let's just get you well, OK?" Carly added. "I just want you to put all this stuff behind you so we can go back to doing things like we always did."

"That sure would be nice."

"But maybe it wouldn't hurt for you to give me a bit of parting advice."

"Such as?"

"Well, anything you can tell me by way of a profile of our killer."

Lyle thought for a moment.

"Honestly, Carly, I can't think of anything we haven't talked about already. We're sure this guy is no sadist. He doesn't want to inflict pain on his victims. And he might have some kind of affinity for grieving people. Like you said yourself, maybe he thinks of himself as an angel of mercy, like he's putting unhappy people out of their misery."

"Which means he's not likely to look or act like a psychotic killer in regular life," Carly added.

"That's right. He might even be quite charming and solicitous. I know that's not very helpful. He doesn't match the usual patterns, so it's hard to even estimate his age and background."

"That's OK," Carly said with a chuckle. "If serial killers hung signs around their necks that said 'homicidal maniac' and they foamed at the mouth like rabid dogs, it would make our job too easy, wouldn't it?"

Lyle chuckled as well.

"Yeah, it would sure put a damper on the thrill of the hunt," he said. "Well, I'd better go now. But don't you go getting into any trouble before George Allen arrives, do you hear?"

Carly laughed some more.

"Hey, I'm just on my way to see the coroner, not to make an arrest. It's probably the last thing I do before Agent Allen gets here. Then we'll probably have to pull a very-late-nighter to get him up to speed."

"OK, then. Goodbye for now."

"'Bye."

They ended the call, and Lyle lay there staring at the ceiling. It felt good to know George Allen would be joining Carly soon. Lyle had real respect for that agent's abilities.

Better yet, he thought sadly, *Allen doesn't have problems with pills or booze.*

She's really better off.

As long as she stays out of trouble ...

As he lay there with his eyes wide open, he realized that was the thing that really worried him.

*

Carly got out of her parked vehicle and walked toward the Lenawha County Coroner building, right next door to City Hall. The street in front of the two buildings was spookily quiet and apparently deserted, like pretty much everywhere else in Harmonium at night.

She rang the front bell, and in a matter of seconds she was greeted by Dr. Russo's ruddy, cheerful face. As he opened the door, Carly saw that he was wearing his hairnet and an apron stained with blood and bits of entrails.

"Come on in!" Russo said cheerfully, stepping aside for her. "I'm sorry for my appearance."

"It looks like I caught you in the middle of something," she replied, walking into the front office.

"Nothing I can't spare a few minutes away from. The dead can be amazingly patient and accommodating—and considerate, too. I wish I could say the same thing about the living."

Carly smiled at his wry comment.

"There's some truth to that, I guess," she said.

"Where is your partner?"

Carly gulped anxiously. She didn't want to get into all that with him.

"Uh, Agent Ramsey is on his way back to Quantico," she said, aware that she sounded rather evasive. "He had—other matters to attend to. Another special agent is on his way to work on the investigation."

"Oh," Russo said with a nod.

His squint made Carly uneasy, as if he could see that she wasn't telling the whole truth. He seemed like a perceptive man as well as a kind one. Fortunately, he also seemed to be able to mind his own business.

"What can I do for you?" Russo asked.

"Dr. Russo, do you have Timothy Johnson's body in storage?"

The coroner's eyes twinkled with curiosity.

"You mean the unfortunate elderly gentleman who died in that awful car wreck? As a matter of fact, I'm just now finishing his autopsy. Why do you ask?"

Carly hesitated, still stumped to think of any plausible excuse for her errand. Finally she decided to be direct.

"Could I have a look at the body?" she asked.

Russo tilted his head with surprise.

"Well, I can't imagine why you would want to. His family requested an autopsy and I'm happy to do it for them, but there's really no question that Johnson's death was just an accident. He simply lost control of his vehicle and drove off a cliff."

"I understand, but …"

Carly fell silent for a moment.

"It's hard to explain," she said. "Let's just say I sometimes follow up on some pretty unusual hunches. And I think it might really help if I could get a look at his body."

Russo shrugged agreeably.

"Well, I don't see any harm in it," he said. "Follow me."

Carly continued on into the morgue itself, with its refrigeration units and its operating table and its chilly scent of formaldehyde.

A body covered with a white sheet lay on the stainless steel table.

"I'm afraid this isn't going to be pretty," Russo said as he pulled back the sheet.

Carly stifled a slight gasp. As accustomed as she was to seeing corpses, this one was in an unusually shocking condition. The face had been crushed to the point where it hardly looked like a human face at all, the chest had been mashed in as well.

Carly could see, though, that Russo really was just about through with his autopsy. There was a huge Y-shaped scar stitched up over the dead man's chest and abdomen.

"The man's widow came in to identify the body the day before yesterday," he said.

"How … how did she …?"

"Identify him? Well, not by his face, obviously. But she remembered certain markings on his body—for example, a mole, and an appendectomy scar from many years ago. The poor woman was terribly distraught. It was no wonder, of course. At least I was able to assure her he died instantly from his injuries."

Russo shook his head and added, "I didn't tell her something that I thought was horribly obvious. The terror he must have experienced when he drove over that cliff must have seemed eternal."

So far, Carly felt no communication from the dead man. She was grateful when Dr. Russo stepped away from the table and busied himself at a side counter.

Maybe if I'm quick and discreet ..."

She lightly brushed her fingers against the man's wrist.

A charge of energy passed through her body from head to toe.

So far, she felt in control of the experience. If she could get a quick message, Russo might only suppose she was standing here in a deep state of thought.

Then she heard the voice she'd heard downtown a little while ago.

"You're here."

"Yes, I'm here," Carly replied with her thoughts.

"Good. Now we can talk. You've got to help her."

"Help who?"

"She's in terrible danger."

"But who do you mean?" Carly asked.

"Aren't you listening? Her life is in danger."

Carly struggled to hear more. Judging from the obituary, more than one woman might be at risk. Like many newly departed spirits, Timothy Johnson was apparently too confused to make himself clear—if he even knew who he meant.

"It's up to you to save her," the spirit said.

"But save who? *Do you mean your wife or your sister or ..."*

Suddenly two spectral voices began clamoring in Carly's head, apparently complaining to Timothy's spirit.

"She doesn't belong here."

"Tell her to leave."

Carly felt a flash of impatience. Why were those spirits interrupting her communications?

To focus better, she closed her eyes.

She was on the ferryboat again, and the voices were coming out of coffins stacked among the craft's dismal funerary cargo. She could see headstones floating in the water.

At the same time, she was anxiously aware that she was still actually standing in the autopsy room with Timothy Johnson's body spread out in front of her, and Dr. Russo was working nearby. She could hear him still rustling around with tools and materials at the counter behind her.

But she didn't want to pull herself out of the vision until she understood what it meant. She recognized the two complaining voices as the spirits of Sarah Tooley and Valerie Irwin, the victims of the second and third murders. Then an equally familiar male voice joined the din, speaking directly to Carly from his own coffin.

"What are you doing here?"

It was the voice of Travis Patten, the man who had been killed under the bridge.

And now all three of the victims were raising a cacophony that completely drowned out Timothy Johnson's spirit, pushing his voice far into the background.

"Be quiet," Carly said with her thoughts. *"I'm trying to talk to Timothy. I need to hear what he's trying to say."*

But the jangled voices continued. Travis Patten was now complaining most noisily.

"This is no place for you."

The women's voices sounded more and more agitated.

"You don't belong here," one of them yelled at Carly.

"You've got to get away from here," the other woman snapped.

"You're not ready to join us."

"It's dangerous for you to be here."

"Dangerous?" she asked.

Suddenly the ferryboat lurched sideways. Water poured over the flat deck, and within seconds the boat sank beneath the surface. Coffins were afloat among the endless headstones poking out of the sea. Carly struggled to swim among the white-capped waves, but the water pulled her under, and as she gasped, her lungs filled up with water.

Her thoughts began to fragment and scatter.

Now she was completely lost.

She had no idea where she really was, only that she seemed to be drowning. Her arms and legs stopped flailing and spread limply in the water. Then she saw a human form in front of her. It, too, seemed to be suspended, with its arms dangling at its sides.

It was a woman, and her hair was streaming in all directions.

My own reflection? Carly wondered.

If so, this was already the strangest vision she'd ever had, as well as the most debilitating. For all she knew, her actual body was lying sprawled at Dr. Russo's feet.

Then a beam of light from above shimmered down into the water, and she saw the other woman's face.

Her skin was pale and lusterless, and her eyes and mouth were wide open.

And slowly Carly realized …

It's not my face.

But it was a face that she recognized from many years past.

Megan!

CHAPTER THIRTY THREE

There was no mistaking that face.

Carly's sister had been a teenager the last time Carly had seen her. Now she looked all grown up, but the face was unmistakably Megan's.

Carly tried to call out, but no words would force their way out of her mouth through the water.

But Megan's lips moved, and she began to speak.

"Poor Carly. You've been looking everywhere for me for all these years, haven't you? You've been frantic—and Mom too, and Dad, and Mark. I'm sorry I went away. You tried to find me, I know. But now ..."

The voice faded for a moment.

Then the pale, deathly face took on an almost blissful expression.

"It's over now, Carly. It's ending right this minute. You don't need to search for me anymore. I'm going away forever, somewhere you can't come to look. But don't worry, I'll be fine. Everything is all right. Everything will always be all right now. Someday you'll understand. Someday we'll be together again."

Her sister's body began to float upward toward the light.

Don't go, Carly tried to scream silently, *Megan, don't go!*

Instead of sound, she felt water pouring up out of her lungs.

She struggled to thrash her arms and legs and try to swim after Megan, but she made no progress, and her feeling of inert helplessness only deepened.

Carly felt overwhelmed by panic. Then suddenly she was coughing uncontrollably, and her eyes snapped open. She found herself in a brightly-lit room.

Where am I?

It took Carly a few moments to remember that this was the autopsy room.

She wasn't in some deadly ocean. She was perfectly dry and seated in a chair. A cadaver was still right there on a nearby table, although she couldn't remember whose body it was.

She vaguely recognized the man sitting in another chair facing her, holding a teacup and saucer.

"Agent See, are you all right?" Dr. Russo asked in a kindly voice.

Carly couldn't reply for a moment. She kept on coughing—although she wasn't coughing up water. She hadn't really drowned.

But somebody else did.

She couldn't quite remember who.

"What—what just happened?" she finally gasped.

"Well, you gave me quite a scare. You fell into some kind of strange state just now. I thought you were going to faint, so I managed to get you seated. It's been several minutes now. Can you tell me what happened? Do you suffer from epilepsy?"

I don't know—do I? Carly wondered.

Everything seemed so strange and unfamiliar. She found it hard to remember even the simplest things about herself. She was dazed and deeply in shock and struggling to make sense of what had just happened. But memories were starting to trickle back, and she heard her sister's voice echoing through her mind.

"I'm going away forever, somewhere you can't come to look."

Suddenly Carly remembered—her sister Megan had reached out to her. Megan had spoken to her.

And because she never received those psychic messages from the living, that could only mean one thing.

It was Megan she had seen drowning.

Carly felt a sob rise up in her throat, then another, then another.

"She's dead," Carly gasped as tears began to pour down her cheeks.

"Who do you mean?" Dr. Russo asked.

Carly cautioned herself not to say anything more. But her grief was too overwhelming. She simply couldn't hold it back.

"My sister. Megan. She's … dead."

Dr. Russo's brow knitted with sympathy and concern.

"I'm sorry to hear that," he said. "When did she die?"

The answer to that question seemed painfully, achingly clear to Carly.

"Just now," she said. "Just … a minute ago."

Dr. Russo's eyes widened with curiosity and he leaned toward her.

"How do you know?" he asked softly.

"I … just know."

A silence fell between them for a moment, then Dr. Russo nodded his head.

"I should have realized," he said with a note of wonder in his voice. "But this is so rare. You can communicate with the dead, can't you?"

Carly felt a shiver pass through her body. This was the first time someone—anyone—had simply called her out about her ability. She wasn't prepared for it, and for a moment she didn't know what to say. She was still trying to wrestle herself out of the grip of her shock and confusion.

"I—I shouldn't talk about it," she finally stammered.

Dr. Russo smiled as he held the teacup and saucer toward her.

"Here, this tea will make you feel better," he said. "It's a special recipe handed down through my family. It will settle your nerves, and at the same time it will perk you right up."

Carly gratefully took the cup and saucer and took a sip. The tea really was delicious. It had a minty taste mingled with a slight tanginess.

"Thank you," she said.

"You're welcome."

Carly's head was still spinning as she continued to sip the tea, and her thoughts were cluttered and jumbled. But she was just coherent enough to realize she'd revealed more about herself than she normally would.

"Um … what I said just now … I didn't really mean …"

But Dr. Russo waved aside Carly's attempted denial with a warm smile.

"It's all right, I understand completely. The world is full of people who don't believe in such things. But I do. I understand. I've known people with your gift before."

"You have?" Carly asked.

"Sure," the coroner chuckled. "Believe me, you meet lots of different kinds of people when you've got a job like mine—including people who have what might be called a special relationship with the dead. But I've never known anyone in your line of work to have it. An FBI profiler! My goodness, that must be—very useful!"

Carly shook her head.

"Nobody knows," she said.

Except for my mother, she thought. But she was too disoriented to try to elaborate.

"Not even your partner?" Dr. Russo asked.

"No, and I … I'm not ready for anyone to know."

"I understand. I won't tell a soul."

Carly felt a swell of rising gratitude as she continued to sip the tea. A soothing silence fell between her and the coroner. Finally Dr. Russo broke the silence in a gentle, compassionate voice.

"Could you tell me … about your sister?"

Carly's throat tightened with emotion. She felt relieved to have a sympathetic ear after such a terrible revelation. Even so, it was still a struggle for her to put her thoughts together.

"She disappeared … many years ago. No one knew where or how or why. And I've … I've been …"

Carly's voice faded as she wiped away her tears with her hand. Dr. Russo handed her a tissue.

"You've been searching for her all these years," he said.

Carly nodded.

"And now you know she's really gone," he said.

Carly nodded again.

"Do you know how it happened?" he asked.

"She … drowned … just now … I think. I don't know how … or where. And I don't know … if I'll ever find out. And even if I do …"

"You won't be able to bring her back."

Carly nodded with a sob and wiped her eyes.

"I can only imagine how devastated you feel," Dr. Russo said. "It must be as though … well, like your whole world has been pulled out from under you."

"Yes, yes, that's exactly how it feels, I …"

Then something began to dawn on her.

"I've got to go," she said. "I've got work to do, I've …"

It took a moment for her remember exactly what work she was talking about.

"I'm working on a murder case," she said.

"That's right," Dr. Russo said. "You came here for some reason having to do with the case; I'm not sure why. Did you think you could communicate with Mr. Johnson's spirit? Did you succeed? Before your contact with your sister, I mean?"

I don't know, did I succeed? Carly wondered.

All she could remember about her experience was a din of voices on the sinking ferryboat and how she'd felt as if she herself had drowned before Megan appeared to her and spoke. She wasn't sure of anything, except the communications had been too chaotic to be helpful.

Still holding the cup and saucer, she tried to get up, but her legs felt terribly wobbly.

"I've got to go," she said. "I've got to stop him before he kills again."

Dr. Russo stood briefly and touched her on the shoulder before she could get to her feet.

"Whoa, you don't want to go rushing off all of a sudden," he said. "Did you drive here?"

Carly nodded as she settled back into the chair.

"Alone?" Dr. Russo asked.

Carly nodded again.

"Well, I can't let you drive, not in your condition, not yet. I'll tell you what, just stay here for a little while longer. Maybe I can drive you wherever you need to go, help you out in some way. In the meantime, try to relax. Finish up your tea. You'll feel better in a moment, I promise. Would you like to lie down?"

"No, I'm fine here," Carly said, fearing that she might fall into a deep, long sleep if she didn't try to stay alert.

"Are you sure? There's a couch in the front office."

"No, really, I'm OK."

"All right then."

For a moment, Carly did indeed begin to feel better—clearer-headed, more coherent, more conscious of what had happened, and what she needed to do next. But then a renewed wave of disorientation and dizziness swept over her.

"Oh, my," she murmured.

"Are you all right?"

Carly didn't reply. She raised her hand to her forehead and struggled to stay seated upright. Vaguely, she realized that whatever was coming over her right now wasn't the same thing as the shock she'd just suffered from her vision.

This is different, she thought.

And somehow she sensed that something was deeply wrong.

As the whole world began to spin, she found herself thinking about what Lyle had said about the killer on the phone.

"He might have some kind of affinity for grieving people."

And Carly herself had suggested that he might think of himself as an angel of mercy for the hopelessly bereaved …

Just like I am right now.

Finally, she remembered her recent hunch that the killer was someone who worked in a funeral home, in close proximity with death.

Of course! she thought, staring at Dr. Russo.

But the coroner's kindly face grew blurry and vague, and Carly felt as though the world was slipping away from her.

The tea! she realized.

Her last sensation was of the saucer and cup slipping out of her hand.

And the last thing she heard was the crash of those objects against the linoleum floor.

Then she was aware of nothing at all.

CHAPTER THIRTY FOUR

Dr. Simon Russo stared down at the woman sprawled on the autopsy room floor. He'd just discovered that Special Agent Carly See was very special indeed.

It was true what he'd told her—that he'd come across a few people who'd seemed to be able to contact the dead. He'd even had some glimpses of the netherworld himself, but those had been long ago when he'd been especially distressed by his childhood traumas. Although he'd lost that kind of contact, he was still more at home with the dead than with the living.

And here was a woman whose abilities seemed to surpass any he'd known of before.

What an extraordinary thing, he thought.

It was as if fate had delivered her to his very doorstep.

Of course, her current stupor had nothing to do with fate. It was Russo's own doing. The homemade tea was laced with the depressant GHB—gamma-hydroxybutyric acid. It was a common date-rape drug, although Russo would never have thought of using it for that purpose. He'd been keeping it on hand in case he needed some kind of sedative to subdue one of the beneficiaries of his eternal mercy.

He hadn't needed it until just now.

And it worked extremely well.

Even so, he felt a flash of worry as he looked over the fragments of the cup and saucer the woman had dropped. Quite a lot of the tea had been spilled. Had Agent See gotten a sufficient dose for what he had in mind?

I'd better act fast, he thought.

He also had some important decisions to make. Before the FBI woman's arrival, he'd been planning to finish up his autopsy of Timothy Johnson, then carry out his usual errand of mercy. He would stealthily break into the man's home after his widow had gone to sleep and put her out of her misery.

I'll take care of that tomorrow night, he told himself.

Meanwhile, he couldn't imagine a soul in direr need of his assistance than this poor woman at his feet. After years of futile searching, she'd just this moment witnessed her sister's death in a mystical vision. How could she possibly go on with life after such a terrible revelation?

She can't, he thought.

And now she won't have to.

But Russo felt himself hesitating. Wouldn't it be wonderful to spend some time with her? Couldn't he keep Carly See alive for a little while, and ask her how it felt to do what she could do?

If he simply nursed her back to consciousness and convinced her that she had fainted again, perhaps they could talk together for a while. He could let her return to her hotel, where breaking in would be easy. Then he could slip in and send her off in a manner more palatable to both of them.

But of course, there was another consideration.

He had good reason to kill her right now—a lowlier, more selfish reason that he felt slightly ashamed of. Now that he knew she was psychic, how could he be sure that she wouldn't read his mind? How could he ever be sure that someone he himself had killed wouldn't gossip with her and reveal what he had done?

After all, she'd come to Harmonium specifically to bring him to what the world so misguidedly thought of as justice. Whether she'd known it or not, she'd actually been his pursuer, and he her prey.

The decision was clear, and Russo felt relieved—just a bit guiltily so.

Nothing to be ashamed of, he assured himself.

After all, self-preservation was his right, his necessity, a noble cause of its own. And it was strangely beautiful that, just this once, the imperative for self-preservation coincided so exquisitely with his mission to release unhappy spirits into the hereafter.

He would definitely have to kill her here and now.

It was fortuitous that this encounter had taken place right here in the autopsy room. All alone in the building, he would have no trouble cleaning up the blood from her fatal wound, and he could easily conceal her corpse until he found some way to get permanent rid of it.

It's fate, indeed.

Carly See shifted slightly and let out a long sighing breath.

"So peaceful," Russo murmured aloud, touching her hair gently. "And soon you'll be free from all the troubles you'd ever have to face in life."

He reached into his pocket for the shiny penny had planned to give to Maureen Johnson. He took it out and placed it firmly in Agent See's hand and folded her fingers around it.

"You'll be needing this," he whispered to her.

Then he walked over to his instrument tray to fetch a scalpel.

*

Carly was only dimly aware that something had been pushed into her hand. Then she heard a voice call her name out of the midst of an impenetrable darkness.

"Carly ... Carly ..."

It was a woman's voice, a familiar voice.

Where have I heard that voice before? Carly wondered.

"Carly, you've got to snap out of this."

Snap out of what?

She had no clear recollection of what had happened just a moment before, and no idea where she might actually be right now.

"Who are you?" asked Carly.

"You know," the voice replied.

Carly felt a deep tingle of realization.

Yes, she knew that voice. She'd heard it before—most recently when it had warned her that Lyle might be on the verge of hurting himself.

It was the spirit of Dawn Metcalf.

"Dawn, what do you mean?"

"Open your eyes."

Carly struggled to do as she was told, but her eyelids felt like they were held down by lead weights. When she got her eyelids open, the light hurt her eyes, and her vision was hopelessly blurred.

But then she glimpsed a metallic flash, and she immediately knew what it was.

A scalpel.

It was the blade Dr. Simon Russo had been using to kill his victims. And it seemed to be hurtling toward Carly like a dart in midair.

With a sudden charge of adrenalin, Carly rolled out of the blade's path.

She saw that it was held in a man's hand. She heard the man who wielded it grunt in surprise.

Dawn's voice spoke again, more sharply than before.

"Get up!"

Carly leapt to her feet. Her vision was as unfocused as before, and the world seemed a blur of shapes and colors. But she was able to make out a large form rising up and lunging toward her.

Dr. Russo, Carly realized.

She instinctively lowered her head and rammed it against her assailant. She heard a loud, groaning gasp as he fell heavily away from her, then the clatter of stainless steel and a loud thud as the examination table overturned under Dr. Russo's weight, spilling the dead body onto the linoleum floor.

"Carly, run!" the voice shouted. *"This way!"*

The voice was clearly coming from Carly's left now. She turned and lurched in that direction until she collided with something hard and solid.

A wall, she realized.

Meanwhile, she could hear her adversary growling and struggling to get back on his feet.

Her hands rushed over the hard surface until they came into contact with a horizontal metal bar.

A door handle, she realized.

She pushed the handle, then stumbled through the door. She took a few half-blind steps forward, then the floor seemed to drop out from under her. She felt her body tumbling down several steps. Then she crashed into a heap, her forehead banging against a hard concrete edge.

She almost lost consciousness again.

A stairwell, she realized, struggling against a new wave of confusion.

She'd fallen part of the way down the steps and now lay sprawled on top of them. And what about her pursuer? Had he regained his bearings yet? Would he be upon her before she could get away?

Sure enough, she heard a roaring voice behind her. She flailed her arms in the direction of that voice and made contact with a pair of shoes. Then she felt a large body hurtling over the top of her, followed by a crash and a groan.

I tripped him down the stairs, she realized.

She knew he might recover at any second, and she was in no condition to engage him in a fight. She staggered to her feet and clambered over his writhing body down the rest of the flight of stairs. Then she vaguely saw another door with a horizontal metal handle. As she began to push the door open, she was blasted by a horribly loud and shrill ringing sound.

It's an emergency fire exit, she realized.

The ringing continued as Carly stumbled out into the night air. But her vision was no clearer than before, and the sudden darkness plunged her into a state of renewed confusion.

Worse still, the world was whirling around her, the streetlights darting every which way like Fourth of July sparklers.

Carly couldn't tell where she was. She had already lost her way, and although she could only hear the din of the alarm she knew that Dr. Russo was probably close behind her.

"Help me," she called out to the voice.

"I can't," Dawn said. *"That's all I can do. I've been here too long. It's up to you now. Everything is up to you."*

"No!" Carly called out. "Don't go!"

But she could feel the spirit's presence palpably waning.

And then Dawn Metcalf was gone.

Carly was finding it hard to stay on her feet. She tottered and almost fell, but managed to catch herself before she hit the ground. She kept staggering along as best she could, but for all she knew she might be circling back the way she'd come.

Sure enough, under a streetlight's beam she made out the blurry shape of a male figure.

It's him, she realized.

I'm running right into him.

But then the shadowy figure called out in a familiar voice.

"Carly!"

"Lyle!" Carly cried weakly.

She staggered a few steps farther, then collapsed at her partner's feet. She heard Lyle call out.

"Stop right there or I'll shoot!"

Things were looking a bit sharper now, and Carly could see that Lyle was pointing a gun at someone in the darkness behind her.

Finally Carly realized that her fist was clenched around something round and small. She opened her fingers, and her eyes were able to focus a bit better now, and she could clearly see the penny she'd been clutching all along.

I won't be needing this.

Before she passed out again, Carly tossed the coin away.

CHAPTER THIRTY FIVE

What a crazy scene, Lyle thought as he scanned the chaos outside the city morgue.

Red lights were flashing everywhere he looked, coming from police cars, firetrucks, and other emergency vehicles. The fire department had arrived a few moments after he himself had gotten here, in reply to the alarm that was still ringing in his ears despite the fact that the clamor had been quelled a few minutes ago.

He knew at least one ambulance must be somewhere in all that confusion, and he planned to press the medics into service to take care of Carly.

As he stood watching, Chief Tallarico and a pair of his officers escorted the handcuffed Dr. Simon Russo toward a waiting police van.

And now media vans were turning up, and the mayor had gotten here as well. Lyle figured the mayor and the media would keep each other occupied for a while.

Really wild, Lyle thought.

Lyle turned to look back at his partner, who was sitting on the stoop outside the morgue's fire exit door. To his relief, she seemed more fully conscious now.

A little while ago, he'd had no idea what kind of situation he was about to get himself into. When the shuttle had arrived to take him to the airport, he'd suddenly gotten a hunch about Carly's errand to see the coroner, based on his own assumption that the killer *"might have some kind of affinity for grieving people"* and that he might be *"charming and solicitous."*

Right then it had occurred to him he might well have been describing the coroner himself. But he hadn't seriously imagined that Russo might choose Carly as his next victim. After all, what did she have in common with the other victims?

Even so, Lyle had sent the shuttle on its way to the airport without him. Then he'd been lucky enough to hail one of Harmonium's rare taxicabs, which had brought him here just in time to save Carly's life and put Dr. Russo under arrest.

Lyle still didn't understand exactly what had happened, except that

Dr. Russo had tried to kill Carly. She had somehow managed to trigger the fire alarm, setting off a chain of reactions that brought everyone to the scene.

Carly waved weakly at him. She was obviously coming out from under the influence of whatever drug Dr. Russo had given her.

Lyle walked back toward where she sat smiling slightly at him. He crouched down in front of her.

"We need to get you to a hospital," he said.

The smile disappeared.

"Not on your life," she replied sharply.

"I mean it, Carly. I'm going to go get a medic team to bring a gurney over here and get you into an ambulance."

"Lyle, if you try to put me on a gurney, I'll scream and kick. You'd have to put me into a straitjacket to get me on a gurney. And good luck trying to get me into an ambulance. I'll make such a huge scene it'll get us both kicked out of the FBI."

"But—"

"I'm not kidding, Lyle. I've been helpless enough for one night. I can't stand any more of that."

He felt a sudden surge of sympathy.

I know what she means.

His own debilitating bout of paralysis during their previous case had traumatized him and left him vulnerable to a new addiction. He didn't want Carly to go through anything like that.

"Here comes Tallarico," Carly said, looking past him.

Sure enough, Lyle turned and saw Chief Tallarico approaching, shaking his head in astonishment.

"Simon Russo—I still can't believe it's him," Tallarico said. "I've known him all my life. I'd never have imagined … I'd never have put him on any kind of suspect list. But it's true, there's no doubt about it."

"Has he confessed?" Carly asked.

"Well, it's more of a rant than a confession. But he's not holding anything back, that's for sure. Right now he's spewing some kind of wild story about getting locked up with the corpses in his dad's funeral home, and how it made him feel on intimate terms with the dead. I'd had no idea about any of that. Nobody had any idea …"

Tallarico's voice faded and he shook his head again.

"But he's going to tell us everything, I guess. Maybe more than we even want to know."

Lyle noticed that the mayor was holding forth to a group of

reporters who looked absolutely fascinated with whatever he was telling them.

"Maybe you'd better get over there to make sure Freelander doesn't say anything too crazy," he told Tallarico.

The chief turned and looked, then groaned.

"I don't know how anyone could say anything crazier than the truth—whatever that is, exactly. But you're probably right, I'd better talk to the media too."

He started off, then turned back toward the agents.

"Wouldn't you two care to make some kind of statement?" he asked. "A case-closed comment for the press?"

Lyle and Carly both chuckled.

"Only if it can be brief," Carly said, "and we can drive back to Quantico as soon as we're finished."

"Can't wait to put Harmonium behind you, huh?" Tallarico said. "Believe me, I know just how you feel. One of these days I'm going to get out of this place—someday soon, I hope."

Tallarico put his hands in his pockets.

"I'll tell you what," he told them. "If the two of you talk to the media, then stop by my office to wrap up a few loose ends, you can be on your way out of here in next to no time."

Carly got to her feet. but she was a little shaky and Lyle steadied her with a hand on her arm.

"But first things first," Tallarico added. "Agent See here needs a good looking over from our chief paramedic for his opinion. Deal?"

"Deal," Lyle said swiftly and firmly to forestall any argument from Carly.

His partner groaned with dissatisfaction, but she didn't refuse.

As they followed Tallarico toward the mayor and the reporters, Carly nudged Lyle.

"No gurneys," she grumbled. "No hospitals."

"We'll see."

"I mean it."

Lyle laughed,

"I know," he said.

As they approached the impromptu press session, something surprising dawned on him.

I feel good.

He quickly realized it was simply because he hadn't been powerless this time. His instincts had brought him to the scene where he was desperately needed, and he had succeeded in saving his partner's life.

Not helpless at all.

Maybe now he could put his lingering sense of failure behind him.

Redemption is sweet, he thought.

CHAPTER THIRTY SIX

Carly breathed a sigh of relief as Lyle drove over the bridge across the Lenawha River, and the scattered lights of the dilapidated old city began to fall behind them.

"I hope I never see that place again," she said.

"I hope so too," Lyle replied. "Well, there's probably not much chance of that … unless another serial killer shows up."

"If that happens again, the Bureau can send someone else to Harmonium."

"Agreed. You and me, we've got better days ahead. Maybe a case somewhere with sunshine and beaches. Palm trees would be fine."

The cheerful tone of her partner's voice made Carly feel like giggling. She realized that she was feeling really good, and it wasn't just because the chief paramedic at the crime scene had finally cleared her to leave.

The medic had examined her pretty carefully and was surprised at how well and quickly she'd recovered from whatever Dr. Russo had given her in that tea. The tea had already been taken into forensic evidence and would be tested soon. But the paramedic was pretty sure it had been some kind of date rape drug.

Predictably, he'd wanted to hospitalize Carly overnight for observation. She'd pushed back and so had Lyle. They had promised she'd get immediate medical attention the minute she showed any sign of relapse.

Carly was feeling good because Lyle seemed to be back to something like his normal self. And of course, she understood why that was.

"Thanks for saving my life," she said.

"Don't mention it," he replied with a chuckle. "If I remember right, I owed you one."

"Well, now we're even."

"Yeah. Let's try not getting ourselves killed in the future."

"That would be good."

A companionable silence fell between them as they continued south on the highway that ran along the river. After a few miles passed by quietly, Lyle spoke up again.

"Carly, I know I've been a mess for a few days. But at least I don't think I'm keeping any secrets from you—not anymore. You know I've been bent out of shape because I'm afraid I'll lose you like I lost Dawn."

Carly nodded silently.

She knew the situation was much more complicated than that. She and Lyle were both faced with the conundrum of deciding what they were going to tell Chief Voss about Lyle's condition, and what the consequences of that decision might be. And of course Lyle's recovery wasn't a done deal. It was going to be a process, and Carly would have to be a part of it.

But at least Carly now had a good idea what had been wrong with Lyle all along.

And yet ...

He wasn't the only one who had hidden things from Voss. They had both hidden some aspects of their lives from absolutely everybody, including each other.

She knew that was what Lyle was really getting at.

"I guess I'm not such an open book to you," she said.

"I guess not."

Carly shook her head with a sigh.

"Lyle, I'm sorry about all that. But really, I don't know where to begin."

Lyle laughed loudly.

"How about let's start with something simple. Who is your new boyfriend? How's that going? And don't act surprised. I asked about this yesterday, remember? I knew there was something romantic going on. Did you really think I was going to let it go?"

Carly didn't reply for a moment.

"His name is Mark," she finally said. "And he's not exactly my boyfriend. And it's not exactly a romance."

"Then what is it, exactly?"

"It's up in the air, that's what it is."

"Well, how long are you going to let things go on like this?"

"What do you mean?"

"I mean, when is it going to get *real?"*

"I don't know, Lyle. I don't know if it's even supposed to be real."

Lyle let out a grunt of impatience.

"Well, let me tell you—there's no 'supposed' about it. You're going to *make* it real. You're going to do something about it right now. Right this minute. You're going to get him on the phone and arrange a date—a real date, not some wishy-washy not-quite-a-date, not some 'just good friends' kind of thing. The kind of date that winds up with kissing and God knows what else. The kind of date that turns your life upside down."

Carly felt stunned. She certainly hadn't expected their conversation to take this turn.

"It's kind of late to make a phone call," she protested.

"No it's not. He'll still be up and awake, and you know it."

Carly found herself smiling. She'd barely thought about Mark since she'd received that text message from him earlier today. And now she remembered how much she'd been looking forward to getting together with him while he was still in D.C.

Lyle's right, she thought. *I should call him.*

She got out her cellphone and punched in his number. She was surprised by his flustered tone when he answered.

"Carly, uh, thanks for calling. I was thinking about giving you a call, but I was afraid of interrupting your work, and …"

His voice faded, and Carly felt a chill of pending disappointment.

This is not good.

"We just wrapped up the case, Mark," she said. "Now is fine. What's going on?"

"I'm on my way to the airport. I'm flying back to Currie tonight."

Carly couldn't hold back a startled gasp.

"But what about … ?"

"I've gotten everything I'm going to get out of the convention. And I'm … well I'm turning down that job offer."

For a moment Carly was too shaken to speak.

She remembered how excited Mark had sounded about becoming a partner in a D.C. defense firm. Their future had seemed to be tangled up in that decision.

"Would it be … OK with you if we saw a lot more of each other?" he'd asked.

She hadn't been able to give him a very positive answer to that question.

And now she still wasn't sure what to say.

"Mark, I hope you haven't made this decision because …"

"No, Carly, it's really not because of us. I just realized I'm not ready to pull up my small-town roots and take on such a big change.

Things are very different here in the city. Maybe someday, but not just yet. And besides …"

Mark fell silent for a moment.

"I was putting pressure on you, Carly," he finally said. "I shouldn't have done that. I'm sorry."

"It was no pressure," Carly said.

Of course that wasn't true. She really had felt pressured. But now the pressure was suddenly off …

And how do I feel about that?

"Let's take things slowly, OK?" Mark said. "We can keep some kind of long-distance relationship going. We can take our time … finding out … you know …"

"I know," Carly said. "Have a good trip."

"Thanks. And let's get in touch soon."

"We'll do that."

The call ended, and Carly sat staring at the highway ahead. She glimpsed a compassionate glance from Lyle.

"Maybe that wasn't such a good idea after all," Lyle said in a gentle voice.

"No, it was probably the right thing to do. Just the right timing, in fact."

"So what did he say? No, don't tell me. He wants to take time with things."

Carly surprised herself with a chuckle.

"Sometimes you're uncanny."

"Not as uncanny as you."

A silent fell between them.

"You know, maybe he was right," Lyle finally said. "About taking time, I mean. It's easy to get in a hurry. There are lots of things about you I'm anxious as hell to know … and I haven't been very patient about it. I'm sorry."

Carly felt a lump in her throat. She knew Lyle was letting her off the hook about telling him about her gift—for the moment, at least. She was grateful. But she also know a reckoning was coming due between them.

"I'm so glad to have you in my life, Lyle," she said.

"I'm glad to have you in my life too."

Carly felt a wave of tiredness sweep over her. She closed her eyes and leaned her head against the side window. As soon as she did, she remembered the last words Dawn's spirit had said to her.

"I've been here too long. It's up to you now. Everything is up to you."

It had sounded so final. Had Dawn meant that she was going away for good, and she wouldn't be watching over Lyle anymore? Carly felt a weight of great responsibility at that thought.

Maybe it really is up to me now—and no one else.

She also flashed back to that awful moment when she'd stared into Megan's pale, drowned face.

"You don't need to search for me anymore," Megan had said.

"I'm going away forever, somewhere you can't come to look."

It had seemed so heartbreakingly final.

Megan must be dead.

But somewhere deep down, Carly felt that something about that vision was wrong.

Or incomplete.

Or ...?

There had been an eerie difference in that vision—a contradiction, something Carly didn't understand.

It was as if Megan was somehow both alive and dead at the same time.

That's impossible.

But either way, dead or alive, she knew she needed to find her sister.

NOW AVAILABLE!

NO WAY LEFT
(A Carly See FBI Suspense Thriller—Book 4)

FBI Special Agent—and psychic medium—Carly See sees flashes in her mind of mysterious paintings, somehow connected to their newest serial killer case. Can they help her enter the killer's mind and hunt him down before it's too late? Or will the maddening riddle just lead her astray—and into a killer's arms?

"A brilliant book. I couldn't put it down and I never guessed who the murderer was!"
—Reader review for Only Murder

NO WAY LEFT is book #4 in a chilling new series by #1 bestselling mystery and suspense author Rylie Dark, which begins with NO WAY OUT (book #1).

FBI Special Agent Carly See, a star in the elite BAU unit, hides a terrible secret: she can speak with the dead. The murder of her sister, still unsolved, plunged her life into grief and awakened a new power within her. All of it feels like a curse—until Carly realizes she can harness her new skills to solve cases. But her abilities are unreliable, and Carly must use her brilliant mind to complete the puzzle—all while struggling to keep her secret from her colleagues.

In this game of cat and mouse, it will be a race to figure out what these victims have in common—and who is next on the killer's list.

But will Carly's vision lead her astray?

A page-turning thriller packed with twists and turns, secrets, and harrowing surprises you won't see coming, the CARLY SEE series is a mystery series that will have you on the edge of your seat, endearing you to a brilliant and unique new character and having you turning pages, bleary-eyed, late into the night. Fans of Rachel Caine, Teresa Driscoll and Robert Dugoni are sure to fall in love.

Books #5 and #6 in the series—NO WAY UP and NO WAY TO DIE—are also available.

"I loved this thriller, read it in one sitting. Lots of twists and turns and I didn't guess the
culprit at all… Already pre-ordered the second!"
—Reader review for Only Murder

"This book takes off with a bang… An excellent read, and I'm looking forward to the next book!"
—Reader review for SEE HER RUN

"Fantastic book! It was hard to put down. I can't wait to see what happens next!"
—Reader review for SEE HER RUN

"The twists and turns kept coming. Can't wait to read the next book!"
—Reader review for SEE HER RUN

"A must-read if you enjoy action-packed stories with good plots!"
—Reader review for SEE HER RUN

"I really like this author and this series starts with a bang. It will keep you turning the pages till the end of the book and wanting more."
—Reader review for SEE HER RUN

"I can't say enough about this author! How about 'out of this world'! This author is going to go far!"
—Reader review for ONLY MURDER

"I really enjoyed this book… The characters were alive, and the twists and turns were great. It will keep you reading till the end and leave you wanting more."
—Reader review for NO WAY OUT

"This is an author that I highly recommend. Her books will have you begging for more."

—Reader review for NO WAY OUT

Rylie Dark

Bestselling author Rylie Dark is author of the SADIE PRICE FBI SUSPENSE THRILLER series, comprising six books (and counting); the MIA NORTH FBI SUSPENSE THRILLER series, comprising six books (and counting); the CARLY SEE FBI SUSPENSE THRILLER, comprising six books (and counting); and the MORGAN STARK FBI SUSPENSE THRILLER, comprising three books (and counting).

An avid reader and lifelong fan of the mystery and thriller genres, Rylie loves to hear from you, so please feel free to visit www.ryliedark.com to learn more and stay in touch.

BOOKS BY RYLIE DARK

SADIE PRICE FBI SUSPENSE THRILLER
ONLY MURDER (Book #1)
ONLY RAGE (Book #2)
ONLY HIS (Book #3)
ONLY ONCE (Book #4)
ONLY SPITE (Book #5)
ONLY MADNESS (Book #6)

MIA NORTH FBI SUSPENSE THRILLER
SEE HER RUN (Book #1)
SEE HER HIDE (Book #2)
SEE HER SCREAM (Book #3)
SEE HER VANISH (Book #4)
SEE HER GONE (Book #5)
SEE HER DEAD (Book #6)

CARLY SEE FBI SUSPENSE THRILLER
NO WAY OUT (Book #1)
NO WAY BACK (Book #2)
NO WAY HOME (Book #3)
NO WAY LEFT (Book #4)
NO WAY UP (Book #5)
NO WAY TO DIE (Book #6)

MORGAN STARK FBI SUSPENSE THRILLER
TOO LATE (Book #1)
TOO CLOSE (Book #2)
TOO FAR GONE (Book #3)

www.ingramcontent.com/pod-product-compliance
Lightning Source LLC
Chambersburg PA
CBHW030617310726
48979CB00003B/755

* 9 7 8 1 0 9 4 3 9 5 2 5 8 *